**PURE
SLUSH
BOOKS**

THe SHiT LiSt

PuRe SLuSH VoL. 16

First published as a collection January 2020
Content copyright © Pure Slush Books and individual authors
Edited by Matt Potter

BP#00085

Pure Slush Books
32 Meredith Street
Sefton Park SA 5083
Australia

Email: edpureslush@live.com.au
Website: https://pureslush.com/
Store: https://pureslush.com/store/

Cover design copyright © Matt Potter

ISBN: 978-1-925536-90-4

Also available as an eBook
ISBN: 978-1-925536-91-1

A note on differences in punctuation and spelling

Pure Slush Books proudly features writers from all over the English-speaking world. Some speak and write English as their first language, while for others, it's their second or third or even fourth language. Naturally, across all versions of English, there are differences in punctuation and spelling, and even in meaning. These differences are reflected in the work *Pure Slush Books* publishes, and they account for any differences in punctuation, spelling and meaning found within these pages.

Pure Slush Books is a member of the
Bequem Publishing collective
http://www.bequempublishing.com/

Stories by

Jane Andrews · Jim Bell

Claudia Bierschenk · Howard Brown

Shanique Burton · William Butler

Chuka Susan Chesney · Rachael Dickzen

Tom Fegan · S. P. Gottlieb

Samuel Gulliksson · Chris Hall

Robin Hillard · Jenna Hillhouse

Kathryn Hood · Mary Krakow

Mike Lewis-Beck · Vickie J. Litten

Patience Mackarness · Sally-Anne Macomber

Lance Manion · Jan McCarthy

Keira Morgan · Christopher Muscato

Edward Andrew Parks · Matt Potter

Melisa Quigley · David Rae

Bruno Rodriguez · Holly Saiki

Jessica Schneider · Beatriz Seelaender

Tim Thompson · Michael Webb

Benjamin Whitaker · Gary Zenker

originally published in
The Quonsettville Quacker, April 3rd 2008

NEW CHIEF LIBRARIAN APPOINTED

by Local Political Reporter, Merriweather Rosenschultz

Following the sudden passing of Chief Librarian Mrs. Florenza Fayette (aged 88) in a fly fishing accident on Quonsett Pond in March, the Town has appointed a new Chief Librarian.

The appointee is Mrs. Euphoria Rivers. Mrs. Rivers and her husband P.P. will return to live in the Rivers' family home on W. Robespierre Street in Quonsett Cascade as early as next week.

"I am honored to be appointed to the role so ably filled by Florenza Fayette," said the new appointee. "And I am looking forward to seeing old friends."

Mrs. Fayette served Quonsettville for over forty years as our chief librarian.

"I can only hope to equal Mrs. Fayette's years of service and her great accomplishment," added Mrs. Rivers.

Born and raised in Quonsettville, Mrs. Rivers and her husband have lived, for the past thirty-six years, in Burlington.

Mr. Rivers worked in the accounts department of the Perseverance Nursing Home, but has plans to "kick back and enjoy the scenery," his wife said.

"I am a direct descendant of town founder Théophile LaChute," Mrs. Rivers said, "so returning to live in Quonsettville will really be returning home for me."

Burlingtonians will miss the popular couple, and Mrs. Rivers has already handed over the reins of her ballet school to her daughter, Mrs. Cissy Stepp. Established in 1979, the Li'l Twirler Dance Academy is one of Burlington's most popular for aspiring ballerinas.

Many Quonsettvillians will remember Mrs. Rivers' late father, Valerian Dubonnet, who served as Town Clerk from 1956 to 1982. Mrs. Rivers' late mother, Ellen Bertoli Dubonnet, was one of our town's most popular hostesses.

When asked what will she institute as Chief Librarian, Mrs. Rivers said, "Florenza Fayette left a wonderful legacy. But change is not necessarily a bad thing."

You can find Mrs. Rivers behind the desk at the Quonsettville Municipal Library from Monday April 14th.

One Fine June Morning

Matt Potter

I don't get a lot of letters any more. And not usually in pink envelopes, with scalloped edges on the back where you stick down the flap with spit and run your fingers along to stamp it down.

"You got a letter," Bernice said, as I dropped my keys on my desk and sat down in my swivel chair. "You don't see much of them any more."

That's Bernice for you, making friends with the obvious.

"You get a lot of emails," she said, tilting back in her own chair, the backrest creaking and the spring straining under the seat. "But not a lot of *mail* mail."

"I know," I said, my hands warm on the leatherette armrests. "Plays havoc with the folk interested in philately." I stared at the letter propped up on my keyboard.

The chair spring snapped under Bernice as she sat forward again. "There you go," she said, turning her pale green eyes on me now, "always using those big words no one understands." She scratched at that rash on her neck and glanced at the letter.

I looked at her pudgy face framed by that mess of gray curls and clamped my mouth shut.

Then I looked back at the envelope.

The writing was small but pressed deep into the pink paper. Was it perfumed? That could just be the sweet cloying stuff Bernice likes to wear. I picked up the envelope, held it to my nose, and sniffed.

"Any notion who sent it?"

Definitely perfumed. Though just a hint of scent, not strong, not like it was dipped in a tub of the stuff. So given the sloping, graceful hand of the writer, probably a woman, of some class.

"They used your full name," Bernice said. "So they must know you."

Mr. Harlequin Pontchartrain, I read on the envelope.

"Probably a local."

Not *Harley*, like on my business card and my email signature and the nameplate on my desk.

"Probably known you a long time, maybe even your whole life."

Most likely a local, willing to make a bold (given the way the envelope was addressed) but also delicate (given the pink paper) statement.

"Check the address on the back," Bernice said, like she'd already checked it herself when she slotted the envelope into my keyboard. "I'm sure it must be local."

I looked at the address on the front again.

Mr. Harlequin Pontchartrain,
Editor-in-Chief,
The Quonsettville Quacker,
230 LaChute St,
QUONSETTVILLE

Then I flipped it to the back.
Just an address.

105 W. Robespierre St,
QUONSETT CASCADE

So from the classy side of town.

"Aren't you going to open it?" Bernice asked. "The suspense must be killing you."

I opened the top drawer of my desk, dropped the envelope inside, and slid the drawer shut.

"There you go like always," Bernice said, chair creaking as she staggered up, "clogging up the channels of communication."

I watched as she waddled past my desk, off to the ladies' room like she goes every half hour. Stopping beside my nameplate, she glared at it, then snorted.

"And you call yourself a newspaperman."

*

I didn't tell Bernice then and I haven't told her still. But later, after she looked at me sideways while side-stepping out the door twenty minutes late for her Thursday lunchtime quilt-making class at the Homemakers' Institute, I slid a letter-opener under the corner of the envelope. And let me tell you: that classy feeling brought on by that pink paper and those scalloped edges and the fancy perfume? That was blown clear out of the water, clear across Quonsett Pond, and came to a rattling halt somewhere way over the Canadian border.

Tuesday, June 11th 2019
I am through with this town and the entire state of Vermont, the letter began, *so I thought you as editor-in-chief of the local newspaper should know why I have left.*

The letter-opener clanged onto my keyboard but my eyes were glued to the curly script.

After 11 years as Municipal Chief Librarian, after 6 years at the helm of the Quonsettville Poetry Appreciation Society, after 8 years as the

Vice-President-of-Everything-Else-That-Nobody-Else-Wants-To-Do with the Quonsettville Historical Preservation League, and after too many years of involvement with too many other committees and groups and working bees to mention, I am quitting.

When you receive this letter, Lord knows where I will be, but I promise you and the 6,872 other inhabitants of this sorry town one thing: I will never return!!

On the back of this letter – and here is where I flipped the letter over, then flipped it back – *is a list of every person in this town who has made my life a living hell and driven me away.*

Yours truthfully,

Euphoria Rivers, M.L.I.S. and former Quonsettville Municipal Chief Librarian

Turning the page over again, I saw it, a list – a long list in tiny, determined print – with many names and their occupations but no reason for their inclusion.

And at the top of the page, in thick letters pressed deep into the pink paper, underlined and in blue ink, were the words: *The Shitlist.*

The Shitlist.

Delmar H. Dickerson · tradesman

Tristan Wheeler · ceramist

Rich Evans · pharmacist

Carrie-Ann Dunlap · beauty salon owner

Florry Fayette · library volunteer

Claudette Cloutier · Fourway Corner assistant librarian

Labette Luricoix · school administrator

Darlene · Tipsey Towhee bartender

Hubris Braggadocio · retired history professor

Dexter Nail · second-rate handyman & pool room lackey

Estelle Burgstaller · accompanist

Dayman de Malville · rude and reprehensible teen

Taylor de Malville · miscreant mother

Frank Hauser · construction worker

Ninette Nebulouse · arts agitator

Henry Devereux · retired high school English teacher

Bambi Chaste · Miss Quonsettville 1969

Agatha Mignonette & Jaxie Molina · horrendous schoolgirls

Chester Franklin · pedantic bureaucrat

"Buddy" Hunt · activist veteran

Neveah Warner · Beatrix Potter fan

Angus and Jasper Tipton · electrician and dog

Dwayne Hoffell · reckless father & amateur woodworker

Travis Johnson · irresponsible Boy Scout

Bethany Lorell · dog groomer

Eve Durrant · student and book-lover

Clifford Redsockett · owner of Bait and Take Marina

Clifford Redsockett Jr. · son of Clifford Redsockett

Gaston Nadeau · owner, defunct Fat Springs General Store

Barton Clamp · Chair, Quonsettville Library Trustees

Jean-Pierre Pelletier · tanner and survivalist

Tyson Kellogg · butcher

Theresa Kellogg · Tyson's daughter

Loretta Lane LaBiché · bakeshop owner

Salome Sullivan · postmistress

Orville Hanson · retired Elvis Presley impersonator

Margot Fontenot Patout · alleged ballet mistress

Gil Burnett · fishing guide

Wiley Pescatoria · charter boat charlatan

Gordon Garfield · inexpert plumber

Pastor Michael Burton · Redeemer Bible Church pastor

Valletta Vale · dark arts practitioner and teacher

The Confession of Delmar H. Dickerson

Jan McCarthy

overheard at the Smugglers' Hole Inn, New Year's Eve 2018

After ol' Hurricane Irene hit Quonsettville in 2011, I had more work than I could handle. Of course the old money and the new got their homes done first, which made no sense to me because they're generally well kept up and solid, with open ground around them so the trees that fell never touched them at all and high enough up to escape the water. And if not, they could afford to put their valuables in storage and go stay in a decent motel further south till people like me had set their houses straight.

My first job was up at the Rivers' place and when I got there I almost turned myself around and went back into town for a beer. What's a few broken windows and a tumbled-down kind of conservatory-cum-shed she reckoned was her writing studio, compared to what a lot of folks were dealing with, myself included? There wasn't much left of my home. Water got in underneath, washed half of it away and the rest slipped sideways into the gully. Had to move in with my sister who at least had her walls still standing, roof still just about sound. Still haven't gotten around to fixing the place up again like it was before. Been helping my brother-in-law Silas instead. You got to keep your drinking buddies sweet.

Preston Rivers – P.P. as he likes to be called – had gone off to Burlington to drum up some emergency funding like the good old boy he is, but Mrs. Rivers – Euphoria – was around and giving orders, like we didn't know our job. I learnt carpentry from my daddy and granddaddy and there's nothing about the trade I don't know. Never took to that woman. Too high and mighty by a long shot. She and P.P. have been away from Quonsettville most of their lives by my count, so why they gave her that job and let her muscle in to the town's business I will never understand.

I got the work done real quick. Never a cup of coffee offered or a sit-down. Went to the lady of the house to get my money, drove back to town, spent the rest of the afternoon drinking, like I always do to stop myself feeling so stirred up. Can never usually sleep at my sister's place, due to the comings and goings to the bathroom in the night, but I slept like a log that night and woke up with an idea in my head that wouldn't go away.

Euphoria Rivers ran just about everything in town by 2011, and what she didn't run, she shook up till folks were going around like they'd been hit over the head. Brought more confusion and panic than Irene herself. But I knew what she had put her heart into, more than anything, and that was the library where they put her in charge. It was her pride and joy, and heaven knows why, because what use are books once you've learned enough to make a living?

The woman was already in trouble with the Poetry Appreciation Society for bringing in what my sister said people were calling *dirty poems* with rude words and ess-ee-ex and stuff, so her morals had already been called into question. Folks said it was living in the city that had ruined her, and that women shouldn't get too much education anyways, that they're better off keeping to home-making and raising kids and patchwork quilting which is what my sister does once a week and has made more than enough to keep the whole family warm in winter. So I took a trip to the library as soon as I had a free afternoon, which I hadn't done since fifth grade, and had a look around. Dark enough in there now Mrs. Rivers has had the strip lighting taken out and old-style lamps with shades put back. Easy enough to do what I had planned which would get the Chief Librarian drummed out of town quicker than you can say Jack Rabbit. Well, it took a little longer than that. But thankfully I wasn't the only one trying to get rid of her.

Euphemism, which is a joke name I call her, though not to her face, was seated at her desk mending books. I took a good look at her through a gap between two books on fly fishing. She looked up and saw me, so I took one of the books to the desk and she stamped it for me and asked if I'd ever done any fly fishing before.

"No ma'am," I said, "I only ever done fishing for fish before."

That made her laugh, a horrible noise like a rusty grating, but at least I'd broken the ice.

"Never had you down for a wit!" she remarked.

She wouldn't. Not an artisan like me, all brawn. They forget you need brains to do the kind of work I do. But I let it go. I made sure to thank her for her trouble, and ask if the work I'd done on her house was satisfactory, and how was her husband and was he back home yet, and we carried on talking for a while like old friends, which was what I'd intended. Smile on my face, concealed weapon behind my back, and now it's time to come to telling you all how I planned to bring her down.

I inherited more than manual skills from my daddy and granddaddy. I inherited the house, a weathered old thing that had been built room by room as was needed and all from the forest that goes with the property. Nothing grand, but useful. And something else: a need for personal space and peace and quiet. My granddaddy never married. Got my daddy on a woman who kept the fire lit and hot meals ready for him one winter while he was recovering from an accident with an axe that cost him the outwards three fingers of his left hand. She moved on, leaving my daddy behind and Granddaddy Cornelius to raise him.

My daddy Culver grew up in a quiet house, as he often used to remind me with a cuff upside the head when I was a boy and liked to line up the pots and skillets and play drums with a spoon along to Elvis on the kitchen radio, and the thought of a woman coming to spoil his lifestyle of choice didn't appeal, any more than it did to my granddaddy. My ma was some rich girl from Montpelier who spent the summer with her aunt, got frisky on a picnic with my daddy and got turned out by her folks till I was born in the convent. The nuns would have had me adopted, I guess. I only know where I was born because my daddy got my birth certificate from there when he needed it later to register me for school. My ma came and dumped me on the front stoop with a note I still have in the bureau that says:

"He's your problem now. I'm going to San Francisco, get some sun in my bones, make a new life for myself. It was nice knowing you, you bastard."

I stray from the subject. The other thing I inherited was a whole stack of porn books and magazines, on account of the menfolk of my family not having recourse to the ladies that much. When Irene hit the house, they were the one thing that never got damaged as I had them under lock and key in a steel cabinet. The solution to the Mrs. Rivers situation and what has made me the savior of Quonsettville is this. I took them down to the library a few at a time and slid them in between the other books in just about every section from Arabic Studies to Zoology.

There were some choice titles that were hard to let go of – well-thumbed, you know, old favorites – and some that were over a hundred years old, like 'The Mysteries of Verbena House, or Miss Bellasis, Birched for Thieving' and 'The Whippingham Papers' that were properly bound and tooled in gold so it was a while before anyone found them and thought to put in a complaint. Women, I guess. Or should I say, ladies?

Mrs. Rivers closed down the library over the weekend and had a clear-out, but I was drip-feeding them and still had plenty left.

Last time I saw her, she was looking frazzled. Stopped her in the street and asked her if everything was OK.

"Ah, Mr. Wit!" she said, giving me a smile that cost her a lot of effort. "Are you enjoying your fly fishing?"

"Yep," I said, "You bet. Caught myself a fine fat one just the other day."

Potty Mouth

Tim Thompson

Tuesday, May 28th 2019:

Henriette De Poset (Posey to her friends) marvelled at the way Tristan worked clay, his ability to turn the spinning brown lump into a delicate work of art. After almost eleven years of being his PA, his promoter, his … voice, she still wondered *how* he did it.

She was watching him from the open doorway to his studio. He hadn't noticed her, or, if he had, he hadn't acknowledged the fact; the clay was all consuming … so much so, it swallowed his Tourette's.

Tristan could feel Posey watching him in the same way he could feel a tic coming on … like waiting for an automatic kettle to click off when the water started boiling … except with Tourette's, it was a click *on*. For Tristan, it meant blinking – the kind that would involve all the muscles around his eyes, not just his lids; it meant jerking his head to the right, like he was trying to dislodge something from his ear, and, worst of all, it meant Coprolalia … only 10% of Tourette's sufferers had it … the utterance of obscenities.

Posey had first knocked on Tristan's door on August 18, 2008 armed with her admiration and a recently acquired marketing degree (specialising in art) from UVM. She'd even been wearing her green and gold college sweater. She would never forget his first words: *Fuck face bitch.*

However, she was just what Tristan had been looking for: an intermediary between him and his clients, who, at that time, were the owner of a boutique homewares store on LaChute Street and an art dealer in Burlington (where Posey had been introduced to Tristan's work).

Tristan gently squeezed the elephant-ear sponge, moistening the clay as he smoothed a scraper across the surface of a vase he was shaping on his wheel. He didn't want to hear Posey's bad news. Tristan lived a life of seclusion, divorced from Quonsettville's uptight, inbred community ... and that included his parents.

Rickard Wheeler was the closest thing to a current-day celebrity Quonsettville had. He owned the John Deere dealership, and for as long as Tristan could remember, his father had been on TV and radio yelling at people to 'Get a Wheeler deal'. Many had done just that, which had made him wealthy enough to buy Tristan a house on the south side of the Quackquois River a mile up from Quonsett Pond ... a modest home, set on two acres with almost 100 yards of river frontage hidden behind a copse of river birch ... out of the way, where Rickard Wheeler wanted his son. Tristan had been happy to oblige.

Now, 22 years later, he was no longer just a talented potter selling his wares on commission and relying on his father's 'embarrassment money', he was the new fashion in high-end homeware art.

Posey was in awe of Tristan's talent, and proud of what she had achieved for him over the last ten years – Tristan's renown had spread across New England and even into Montreal, and she'd just established his work in exclusive stores in New York and Chicago. Everyone who was anyone was now buying Potty Mouth.

Tristan smoothed out the lip of the vase. Posey was the only person, apart from his late grandmother, who could put him at ease. She was responsible for … well, just about everything good that had happened in his life since his grandmother had died in a fly fishing accident eleven years ago.

He still missed Florenza; she'd introduced him to pottery. She'd also bequeathed him $500,000 in her will, allowing him to repay his father, build a new studio and employ Posey.

But more than anything, Florenza had been the only person in Quonsettville to truly accept his Tourette's, and always welcomed him in the library. She once told him: "You're lucky, Tristan; your body rids itself of frustration, *ours* festers inside us." Then she'd smiled. "Oh, to swear with impunity – Quonsettville is full of fuck face bitches and bastard motherfuckers."

Posey watched a smile form on Tristan's face; the clay really did transport him to another place. Posey wasn't looking forward to bringing him back to reality.

She hadn't met Euphoria Rivers until today; Tristan hadn't talked to "the preening hag *fuck face bitch*" since she'd banned him from the Municipal Library on April 15, 2008 – Euphoria's second day as Chief Librarian and only a month after his grandmother's death. It had been bad enough recently receiving the fine of $1,278.50 (signed by Euphoria Rivers on the 11th anniversary of his ban) for three overdue books. Posey dared not think how Tristan would react to Euphoria's latest demand.

Tristan placed the scraper back in its holder, squeezed out the elephant sponge and reluctantly switched off the wheel. It was time to put another wheel in motion.

He'd ignored the fine, thinking it must be some kind of bad joke or belated last word… eleven fucking years after the event! Then, two weeks ago, Posey had received another letter, this time from a Burlington law firm, LeBeau Deschamps, representing the interests of Quonsettville Municipal Library on behalf of the Municipal Chief Librarian.

He'd wanted to confront Euphoria, but Posey had been the voice of reason, convincing him to allow her to act on his behalf. "Let me talk to her; we may be able to turn it to our benefit."

The voice of reason was now regarding him from the studio doorway with a look of resignation.

Posey had dealt with many anally-retentive snobs in establishing Potty Mouth, but none came close to Euphoria Rivers. She'd arranged the meeting with Euphoria after three phone calls and four emails… Posey had, at first, been directed to Sebastien LeBeau; it was a legal matter, and all correspondence was to go through him, but she'd managed to convince Euphoria that her intentions were conciliatory.

Posey had felt upbeat walking into the library. However, what she hadn't expected was Euphoria's uncompromising determination to see the fee paid – in person – by Tristan.

Tristan's blinking and head jerks started as soon as the wheel slowed. "I take it she wasn't agreeable, *fuck face bitch?*"

Posey shook her head.

*

Approaching the Municipal Library was less confronting than Tristan imagined. As he walked past the statue of Théophile LaChute, up the steps to the automatic glass-doors, the midday sun flared against the steel hand-rail of the disabled access. A poster near the door depicted people from a myriad of ethnicities (one was in a wheelchair) with the caption: 'Books are bound. Reading is boundless.' Tristan acknowledged the irony with a jerk of his head and a loud *"Fuck face bitch!"*

His tics increased as he entered the library. Only a smattering of people studied at desks or gazed at shelves, which just made Tristan even more of a focal point as he walked towards the library's front desk.

He didn't recognise the woman sitting behind the desk, but she wore an expression Tristan was *very* familiar with. His Coprolalia kettle was beginning to boil, but he managed to eke out a civil "Hello" and asked to see Euphoria Rivers.

"I'll just see if she's available," the woman said, smiling awkwardly. "May I ask your name, sir?"

Tristan told her… just… his head jerked to the right, which sent the librarian hurriedly to a door behind the front desk. The desire to swear was overwhelming. As she opened the door, Tristan yelled out, *"Fuck face bitch fucking bitch fuck!"*

Despite his wishes to the contrary, Posey had followed Tristan to the library. She parked her 2018 Mini Cooper Countryman (blue with white roof and GT stripes) next to his silver

Chevrolet Tahoe. She could see the library's entrance, looking like a disapproving mouth. She waited to see what it spat out.

Euphoria Rivers looked exactly as Tristan remembered her.

"Mr Wheeler." She began without preamble. "I take it you are here to return our books and pay your fine."

In response, it was hard to tell where Tristan's anger finished and the Coprolalia started.

"I'm *not* here to pay your fine *fuckfacebitch*, nor return your books *fuckfuckbitchface*, I'm here to tell you that if I receive one more fucking letter from you or your lawyers *fuckfacebitchfucker* about this fucking fine, then I shall ask my PA, who has *very* good media connections *fuckersfuck* to do all she can to expose your intolerant stewardship *bitchmotherfucker* of a *Municipal* fucking library... you represent everything my grandmother hated about Quonsettville!"

Posey glanced up from her Infotainment display to see Tristan walking down the library steps. He was obviously agitated, his head was jerking rapidly, and even through a heated debate about Mexican immigration on WVPS, she could hear his swearing. She turned the radio off and got out of her car.

Tristan felt exaltation as he exited the library... the sun no longer glared, it shone... he even embraced his Coprolalia; his kettle runneth over with expletives... *"Fuckface fuckersfuck fuckfuckfuckfuckfuck..."*

He stopped when he noticed the blue Mini parked next to his car, and Posey walking slowly towards him. He quickened his pace towards her. She looked worried.

"Are you okay?" she asked.

"*Fuck face bitch!*" he yelled. "Never felt better."

Dear Prudence

Michael Webb

I watch Pru, her gold hair clip bobbing up and down as she cleans up the mess. A still pudgy new mother has dislodged some shampoo with a swing of her shoulder bag, and Pru has rushed over to help restore order.

Her parents named her Prudence, presumably after the Beatles song, although I have never asked her. As names do, it has come to suit her – quiet, calm, serious, barely registering the storms of late adolescence. She only takes steps after considering them first, an attitude that explains her excellent employment record and her avoidance of the pitfalls of what pass for Quonsettville's rough crowd. She stands, her mop of brilliant red hair tossed back onto her shoulders with a gesture I'm sure has made Quonsettville boys, and not a few men, catch their breath. She is going to be a freshman at Smith College in the fall, and while I've really had nothing to do with it, I feel proud of her anyway.

The door of the Quonsettville Pharmacy swings open, and it is Euphoria Rivers who comes in, her cheeks already flushed. I know Euphoria, the chief librarian – it is hard to fail to know, or at least know about, anyone in a town of almost 7000. Since buying this store twenty years ago, gaining a life and losing a marriage, I feel I have seen just about everyone at least once. I vaguely recall Rivers has been in a day or two ago.

"Rich," she begins, her voice already rising. "Your girl charged me $13.79 for this the other day." She shakes a clenched receipt in her hand at me. "It was only $5.27 last time. Why did she charge me so much?"

"Ms. Rivers," I say.

"Euphoria," she cuts in.

"Euphoria," I start again, "She isn't *my girl*. She has a name. And she didn't charge you anything, your insurance company does. I charge what they tell me to charge. We have been through this."

She shakes the receipt again. "Why did she charge me so much?"

Out of the corner of my eye, I can see Pru, her eyes just over the top of the shelf she is now pretending to straighten. Her eyes are vibrant and green, I'm sure another fact that does not go unnoticed by her suitors. A lock of her hair has come loose from the clip, and it hangs across her forehead like a comma.

"Euphoria," I say. "I told you the last time this happened. There are coverage gaps, and tiers, and these are all things that your insurance company can tell you easier than I can."

"But I'm asking *you*," she proclaims. "I'm asking you why she charged me more!"

I raise my voice, something I only do when confronted by the drug-seeking or the belligerent.

"EUPHORIA! Stop it. I know you're an intelligent woman, so I want you to stop yelling at me and listen. These prices come from your insurance, not from me, and certainly not from my employees. Now you have exactly three choices here. You can go home and call your insurance and yell at them. You can admit that I'm right, just pay what they say because that's what you contracted to do, and go about your day like an adult. Or you can drive down 237 until you find a pharmacy that you like yelling at better than me. But what you can't do, what I will *not* accept, is you standing here and yelling at me or my people for something I didn't do!"

No one breathes. I am shocked by my own anger, my fists balled on the counter out of her view, the last words I threw at her hanging in the air. Euphoria's face freezes, trying to register my volume and seriousness, the expression of someone not used to being talked back to. Euphoria turns, and without another word walks back out the door, and we hear her start her Dart, shove it into gear, and I watch it spit some gravel as she pulls out onto LaChute Street.

I am ashamed. I let her push me, and I lost my cool. I don't particularly care if I lose her business, because with all the fees I get charged by her insurance, I barely break even on the blood pressure pills she was so concerned about. Prudence comes forward to the register, and the new mom brings a box of diapers and some ginger ale to the register, where Pru dutifully cashes her out, and we are in the store alone again.

I don't know what to say, so I don't say anything.

"That was weird," Pru finally says.

"Yes, it was," is all I can manage.

Pru returns to her task, sorting and rearranging the candy, tossing out empty boxes, her hair clip glinting in the afternoon sun. She didn't need to be defended, but I did it anyway, and she didn't need to thank me, so she crouched there and focused on her job, probably dreaming of the lesbian poetry seminars and wood-fired pizza her future holds, and I stand there and watch her for a moment longer than I should.

How It Got Out

Bruno Rodriguez

"Here's the proof your name's on that damn list, which you can see with your very own eyes," cousin Bernice said. "I had a hell of a time steaming the letter open; she must've used a ton of extra adhesive glue on that pink envelope."

Bernice shook her head, though her mess of gray curls was a little oily and at the crown stuck straight to her scalp.

"And then I had an even harder time sealing it shut again!"

What treatment would work best on gray, curly, oily hair, I wondered?

"You know how Harley takes his precious job so seriously," she added.

Bernice thrust the paper at me and rustled it in my face.

"But I had just enough time to scan and print it," she chuckled, her beaming face now pudging up. "Damn that pernickety husband o' mine."

"Oh, I don't know, Bernice," I said, clasping my hands against my stomach and twiddling my thumbs. "If Harley has refused to publish it in the *Quacker*, maybe we should follow his lead. Perhaps Euphoria's had time to cool down and regrets her actions. It seems so awfully mean to –"

"Mean mung bean!" Bernice cracked. "It wasn't your fault you had lice in all your brushes and combs. Hell, she probably put them there herself!"

Bernice tossed the list on to the table beside the six-high tower of three-gallon bottles of Major Miracle perming lotion.

"That bitch ruined your business!"

I shrank back against the fresh (and dusty) tower of towels resting beside the wall. "That's all water under the bridge, Bernice, and you know I never like being too busy."

Bernice grabbed the back of a chair. "That's not the point, Carrie-Ann! She accused you of infecting her holy head of hair with lice and that sent Carrie-Ann's Hair Nest – until then the number one beauty salon in Quonsettville – to the wall!"

Bernice released her grip on the chair and scratched at that rash on her neck.

"Which is why you get to spend twelve hours a day here out back of your salon and not out front helping the women of Quonsettville add a little beauty to this town."

She smiled, and pushed a greasy curl behind her ear.

"You deserve your revenge. You weren't the only one she peed on. Which is why I have this little doohickey here."

Bernice stuck her hand into her pocket and pulled out a little gray stub of plastic. She held it up, waving it in mid-air.

"And I bet every one of the eight hundred and twenty-seven households and businesses on this email list here on this USB deserves to know the truth too."

I looked at the floor. I guess Bernice had a point.

The floor was so dusty, too, although none of it was hair; just dirt and probably eastern towhee doo doo. I really should sweep it more, I thought.

"Well," I sighed, "it's true I'm certainly not making a living out of the salon any more. But what if someone finds out the emails are being sent from here?"

"They won't," Bernice said. "It'll be easy. I just have to set up an anonymous gmail account on your computer and then we're on our way."

Bernice grabbed the back of the chair again, pulled it out from under the table and wheeled it over to the computer.

"If I did this at the *Quacker*, Harley would get his snoop on and try to bust my butt," she said, pflomfing into the chair. "Now get me some chamomile tea with three sugars and lotsa milk, 'cos I gotta lotta work to do!"

Poor Bernice, I thought, watching the steam rise as I poured boiling water over the teabag and into the mug. Caught in a loveless marriage with the most decent man in town. He really is so honorable, marrying her because she … well, I'm not sure just why Harley married Bernice, but there you go, maybe he's simply the marrying kind. Just a thoroughly decent man: Harley Pontchartrain, doing good things for no reason at all.

Including refusing to publish that horrible list in the *Quonsettville Quacker*.

"I'm just trying to create a new gmail account here," Bernice told me.

"That's nice," I said, dunking the teabag in the water.

"It's not *nice*," said Bernice, "it's *revenge*. I'm gonna call it quonsettvillewhistleblowers@gmail.com."

"Oh," I said.

Bernice swivelled in the chair to face me. "You don't think it's good?"

"Well," I said, squinting at the milk as I poured it into the swirling mug of yellow tea. "Whistle blowing sounds so …"

"You want me calling it carrieannshairnest@gmail.com? 'Cos I could."

"Well, no, but …" I grabbed the sugar pot from the window sill and opened the lid. "That's three sugars you said you like?"

"Make it five," Bernice said, "it's getting serious."

*

Clunk clunk clunk. Bernice's fingers thumped across the keyboard as she hammered out her message.

I counted the Bright & Beautiful hair dyes standing on the middle shelf above the sink. Sometimes I like to recite them in my head, alphabetically. It passes the time in between not having any customers.

Luckily, that's the way I arranged them.

Alphabetically.

Ash Blond, Ash Blonde, Ashe Blonde, Ashy-blonde, Ash Brown, Ash Brownette, Ash Brunette, then Brunette Ash but really, it should be Brown Ash Brown.

Oh, dear …

I stood up, crossed to the sink again and took down the Brunette Ash bottles because that's where the Brown Ash Brown should really stand, between Ash Brunette and Brunette Ash. But then, out of the corner of my eye, I spied them: sixty-four bottles of Brown-All-Over, on the next shelf to the right. I shook my head, and remembered Mrs Rivers' angry face.

And her open hand with a dead louse on it.

That is the single for lice, isn't it? Louse?

And then I gasped! Oh my, she was sooo angry!

"I'll put you out of business!" she screamed.

"I am not an ogress!" she yelled.

"But how can I support local business when local business continues to fail me?!" she shouted.

I looked at her open hand with the dead louse bouncing on it as she gave me too many pieces of her righteous mind.

"There is a perfectly good beauty salon just opened round the corner from my home on West Robespierre Street and they are offering very generous discounts to new customers!"

After that, I ordered the extra large shipment of sixty-four bottles of Brown-All-Over, kind of like an insurance policy so she would come back and not tell the world about the louse. Or lice.

Because Brown-All-Over was her color, she said, and she made sure that no one else in town wore the same hair color. At least I could do that for her. And no one ever did ask for Bright & Beautiful Brown-All-Over, at least no customer of Carrie-Ann's Hair Nest while Euphoria Rivers was coming in for her two-weekly touch-ups.

Sixty-four bottles of Brown-All-Over.

One lousy louse.

Though last time I saw her on LaChute Street, she was gray-all-over. Which made me kind of sad.

"Hey, Carrie-Ann," said Bernice.

I turned from rearranging the bottles and saw her grinning face.

"Well, I got some bad news and some good news and some bad news and some good news."

She drummed the back of the chair.

"The good news is that eight hundred and twenty-seven households and businesses in Quonsettville now have Euphoria Rivers' scanned shitlist in their email Inboxes. The bad news is that Harley will know it was me who sent the emails because he thinks no one else has seen the letter except him and he'll go apeshit at me when he realizes that I probably steamed that letter open behind his back. Which I did."

Bernice raised her eyes to the ceiling.

"But then the good news is that Harley going apeshit is like being attacked by a gummy bear. But then the bad news is that some people will think it's Harley who sent the anonymous emails, but then most of those people will then realize that Harley would never send emails like that, because he's such a saint. So that's good news. There's probably more bad news and more good news mixed up in there somewhere, but hey, who's counting?"

Bernice laughed.

"So everybody wins," she added, shrugging her shoulders and smiling.

She turned back to the computer to clunk away at the keyboard some more.

"Ha! And some people say nothing ever happens in Quon-settville."

I looked down at her mug of milky, sugary, cold chamomile tea. "You didn't drink your tea."

"Oh, I hate chamomile tea," she chuckled. "And with all that milk, looks like someone peed in it."

She winked at me.

"I just hate people breathing down my neck when I got some serious revenge happening."

And Bernice winked again, pushed another greasy curl behind her ear, and scratched that rash on her neck.

Florry's Perspective … with Soda

Keira Morgan

Ms. Florry Fayette rattled the door handle of the Municipal Public Library for a third time. Stepping back, she removed a neatly ironed handkerchief from her shirt-waist pocket, dried the beads of perspiration on her upper lip, refolded the crisp square and replaced it. Really, this excessive heat. Global warming, presumably. If you believed in such a thing. Like Euphoria did. Where *was* she anyway?

Florry tapped her watch: 12:58 p.m. *She* made it a point to be early. Not like some people she could name. She stepped back to the white porch railing to peer up and down LaChute St. Where *was* Euphoria? Cars idled past, vying for the few angled parking spots not already taken, but none matched Euphoria's clunky, old faded-pink Dodge Dart – the one you could hear coming for blocks – though she might dash up in their new electric car, a bright-red Kia Soul. (She *said* she had to toss a coin with her boys each day to see who got to drive it. What nonsense.) Such fecklessness had *never* been permitted when her dear Godmother, Aunt Florenza, had been in charge. But Euphoria took things so lightly. Really, everyone thought she would do better than Euphoria with the library.

When Bernice mentioned yesterday at quilting that she'd noticed the venetian blinds on the library door were closed when she'd driven past at 4:30 yesterday afternoon, Florry had just said that dear Euphoria had a generous relationship with time. But this was carrying things too far. No wonder the library couldn't keep its volunteers and staff, if it couldn't even open. It was basic, really. She'd mentioned it to Euphoria once or twice. In the kindest way. Teasing. Suggesting Euphoria might want a new alarm. Or that she'd be delighted to serve as a wake-up service. They were the greatest of friends, she and Euphoria, as she told everyone who came in to use the Reference Desk. Known each other since grade school. They'd both moved to experience big city life but they'd both come back to the peaceful life and small-time values that had proven the most solid.

Florry peered at the door again. The venetian blind swayed indolently as if to mock her. Did it truly mean the library hadn't opened since yesterday afternoon? Hearing footsteps tapping up the stairs to the wide white porch, she turned and said, "Mrs. Dubonnet. Are you coming to the library? I'm so sorry. It seems to be closed."

"No, dear. On my way to the municipal office to meet Daniel. The library's closed? And no notice? Dearie me. Hmmm. I wonder ..." She peered up and down the veranda and over her shoulder as if she expected Euphoria to arrive on a broomstick. Not that Florry would be surprised at anything Euphoria might do.

"Why don't you just come along with me?" Mrs. Dubonnet said, taking Florry's arm.

"When my cousin was librarian, volunteers had keys. But Mrs. Rivers has made changes. As is her right, of course. Though I'm not the only one to find it awkward. Not that I'm one to spread gossip. But Bernice – over at the *Quacker* – says the library was closed when she went by at 4:30 yesterday ..."

Mrs. Dubonnet murmured, "Mmmhumm," as they rounded the veranda corner and arrived at the extra-wide colonial doorway. Above their heads the old-fashioned bell tinkled as they pushed open the screen door into the wide, oak-planked hallway carpeted with a dark red runner that continued up the central staircase. No one sat in the reception desk, visible through the open doorway on the left, though a large ceiling fan whirred lazily. The two ladies paused a moment before Mrs. Dubonnet wrenched open the handle on the right-hand door.

The startled gaze of the town clerk, Daniel Dubonnet, met Florry's. Raising his eyebrows, he stood to greet them, almost knocking over his chair. He bumped round the corner of his desk to stick out his hand, giving Florry a flash of his yellowing teeth. How did dumpy Deborah Delibes ever manage to catch so handsome a specimen as Daniel? He could have done better for himself. Gazing at him critically she thought he was aging well. He hadn't lost any of that full, thick head of hair, though it had turned iron gray.

"Ms. Fayette, a delight as always."

Always the politician. "Equally a pleasure. Though I could wish the circumstances were happier." Florry sighed and clasped her hands together under her chin as if praying.

"Florry came to work at the library with Euphoria but it's still locked," his wife inserted as smoothly as an aide handing her minister a file. "She volunteers on Fridays." There was something odd about Mrs. Dubonnet's tone – it seemed minatory rather than anxious. "Perhaps … ?" Her voice trailed away.

As Florry watched, their eyes met and a message passed between them. Daniel reached out and took Florry's hands in both of his. "I'm *so* sorry. I've been remiss. And you are the unfortunate, upstanding citizen of our fine town to suffer my forgetfulness. Mrs. Rivers was … uh … is … unfortunately called away … and unable to open … and uh … I've been so caught up finalizing things for today's budget meeting that I plum forgot. I hope you haven't been waiting out there, in this unseasonable heat too long?" He took out a handkerchief and wiped his forehead.

"She says there's talk over at the *Quacker*, too."

Florry was sure Daniel's shoulders slumped. But she had bigger issues on her mind. "I hope you're not about to include Euphoria's extravagant ideas for all those computer thingees and technical gewgaws she's been on about in your budget, Daniel. I've been telling her we don't need that kind of modern nonsense here in Quonsettville. Look at how it's ruining America. Next thing you know she'll be having the next national televised town hall right here … with Bernie Sanders versus the local Republican in our local town library." She forced a giggle, inviting them to ridicule Euphoria's modern notions along with her. "Why is she always trying to change things? People here don't go along with it."

"Where did you get the notion that she wants to buy new technology, Florry?" The town clerk crossed his arms and settled back against his desk.

"There's been talk, Daniel. There's been talk. Uncle Gene's a Library Trustee. Well, we Fayettes have been involved in the library one way and another just about forever. I've been talking to him – not speaking out of turn – but he's mentioned a few things. My poor auntie's sure to be spinning in her grave with all these goings-on."

"So you don't think Quonsettville is up to facing the big, bad world, Ms. Fayette?

"Nor should it be, Daniel. What we need are places of peace and harmony, like this town. Euphoria is another who thinks as I do. She's been out there, and she came back to the tranquillity here, too. Of course, now and then she gets notions, like this computer thingee, from her studies, but she listens to me and comes round." She hadn't expected to find a benefit in Euphoria's sudden disappearance, but life sometimes dealt a good hand. Florry patted herself on the back for her quick thinking.

"Is that so?" Daniel gave her a small tight smile. He reached behind him. "Perhaps you'd be interested in this." Handing her a copy of a letter, he added, "Bernice over at the *Quacker* showed it to me just this morning."

Florry was spluttering by the time she had finished. As she started to turn it over to the back, he said, "That's a copy. There's nothing on its other side." She felt his eyes on her face. "What do you think of that?"

"Well, I never! Up and gone! She always was ..."

"She's my cousin, remember."

"Didn't *you* put her name up for librarian? But of course, she and I ..."

"Before you say more ..." He held out a second sheet. She lunged for it like a cobra striking. Scanning the list, her face became as red as a cooked lobster as she read the names of the town's most upstanding citizens. But when she came upon her own, Daniel feared he might have to engage in mouth-to-mouth resuscitation.

For a moment she staggered and thought she might actually fall. She'd always been so careful in her dealing with Euphoria. Always spoken nicely to her. Made sure that the criticisms came from others. Really, the whole Rivers clan was extraordinarily oversensitive; always looking for slights where none were intended.

"Well I never," she repeated. "And I was always so *good* to her. But there, I always knew there was something flighty about that woman." Her cheeks burned a fiery red.

"Is that so?" said Daniel. "Well, as the library won't be opening this afternoon and you look as if you've had a bit of a shock, perhaps you'll want to step over to the Quonsett Arms for … what did Douglas Adams call it … ? a drink of perspective and soda."

Claudette's Secret

Mike Lewis-Beck

Claudette sat at a picnic table at the edge of Quonsett Pond. Twilight had come on early, with a splash more orange. The water was black, not blue, and gave off a dank odor. She sat, licking her maple creemee while staring at Harley, who let his creemee dribble down the ridges of the waffle cone. "JJ's makes good ice cream," she said.

"A pretext to lure you here," said Harley, prompted by her Little Red Riding Hood cloak.

"Still holding a torch for me, Harlequin?" They had been 'a number,' even though Claudette had attended St. Everine Catholic Girls Academy while Harley had attended Quonsett-ville High, but Bernice stole him away one moonlight night on a hayride. Harley married Bernice just after his Commencement Speech, 'Press of the Future.' These days Bernice sat at her desk opposite his, doing office chores for the *Quonsettville Quacker.*

"Torch extinguished," Harley answered, despite his despair over Bernice's waddling bottom, cheap perfume, and endless sarcasm about his talent. He was a newspaper man, and a damned good one. To prove it, he was dedicating himself to writing a prize-winning story about the townspeople on Euphoria's Shitlist.

Harley felt that the list itself was symptomatic of the contemporary tensions in small town life, including the 'brain drain' of people like Claudette. Business could be better. Green Mountain Market had to let go its butchers and now just sold pre-packaged cuts. The lone hardware store, Auchon, converted to automated sales clerks last winter. Hogarth Lumber Mill, purveyor of quality furniture wood, had a potential German buyer. Worst for Harley, a civic booster through and through, was the demise of the Quonsettville Community Marching Band. He would miss them on parade the 4th of July.

"Why's your name on the Shitlist?" he asked, smoothing his pomaded hair. A moose nodded approval, then made its backward walk out of the cattails.

"Secrets are like diamonds," said Claudette. Caught by surprise, Harley held his ice cream cone motionless, mouth open. "It's about Florenza Fayette, my diamond and life mentor. She made Quonsettville library the best town library in Vermont. Euphoria made it the worst."

Claudette Cloutier came to Quonsettville from Trois Rivières, Québec at age eight, when her parents decided to set up a food truck vending *poutine* (cheese curds and brown gravy over fries). The *poutine* was popular, but Claudette was not, because her English was poor. She spent free time reading English language books aloud at the library, under the direction of Mrs. Fayette. (Her first serious oral reading was Winnie the Pooh.) They became fast friends, Claudette helping after school at the information desk. When she left to go to university (UVM), she was destined to take a library science degree. Her first job was at Middlebury College, helping curate the Robert Frost collection, but she missed home, and eventually accepted an Assistant Librarian position in Fourway Corner, an easy commute from Quonsettville, where she observed firsthand the library shepherded by her teacher and friend, Florenza.

At the end of Mrs. Florenza Fayette's many years of service as Chief Librarian, its holdings spanned the Dewey Decimal system, over 17,000 shelved books, some 1500 reference works, and almost 100 newspapers. These resources could be accessed by nearly 2000 cardholders who could check out AV equipment, schedule a meeting room, even access a computer with guided instruction. The library rivaled LaChute Community Center as the cultural hub of the Northeast Kingdom. Upon Mrs. Fayette's death, Claudette had hoped to fill her post, but lost out to Euphoria. She had not expected this setback, since Euphoria had not lived in Quonsettville for almost forty years. Nevertheless, she dedicated herself to honor the good works wrought by her library mentor, whom she missed dearly. Wherever Claudette shelved a classic, she would remember how Florenza exclaimed: "That's a choice for the Great Books display!"

Claudette planned to praise Florenza in an official address to the Historical Preservation Society, on the fifth anniversary of her death. Instead, Euphoria, as Vice-President, following her Robert's Rules of Order, tabled indefinitely the operative motion received from Claudette, on grounds it lacked vetting by the Speaker's Committee. (Euphoria was head of the committee.)

Why did Euphoria bury this celebration of Mrs. Fayette? Euphoria wanted the Society to bolster the Musée de Théophile LaChute, town founder, and from whom Euphoria claimed direct descent. Last March, on Town Meeting Day, Euphoria spoke before the Selectboard. She planted her rubber-gripper walkers—worn to teach 'Twinges in the Hinges'—on the polished granite, where the state goddess, Ceres, lay etched. Securing her bread loaf forearms under a pillowed bosom, Euphoria parted her rouge lips, and began: "I have taken the road not taken, as our Robert Frost might say, and returned to my ancestral home to lift a baton grown heavy under the valiant struggles of Chief Librarian Florenza Fayette who, God bless, felt her 88 years. Too, as I reported in our esteemed newspaper the *Quonsettville Quacker*, 'change is not necessarily a bad thing.' I charge you, chosen leaders of this noble community, to refurbish the Musée. How it saddens me to see my great-great-grand-père's tattered Sergeant Major uniform—epaulets dangling, dusty in an ancient glass case. *C'est triste …*"

"Objection!" shouted Claudette from the gallery. The Town Clerk, Cliff Redsockett, who otherwise ran Bait and Take Marina, signaled Claudette to step forward. (He was partial to Claudette. He wanted his son, Clifford Jr., married to her, away from his bobblehead girlfriend Marie-France who, when she wasn't draining sap buckets at Descartes Hollow Farm, was draining Lone Trail longnecks. He recognized Claudette as a catch once he learned she'd inherited Florenza's flyfishing lures.)

"Thank you, Mr. Redsockett," commenced Claudette, from the balcony. Around her she saw faces, some friend and some foe. To fight nerves, she focused on Cliff's face. "LaChute Museum has turned shabby. Mice have gnawed buttons off the costumes, the Civil War toy collection shows only rust, the daguerreotypes of the Pergola are shredding. The guidebook *Low Velocity Vermont* gives tourists this directive about the museum: 'only stop if you must.' Of course, we want travelers to stop here, as we have much to offer. But LaChute Museum, due to its irrelevant state, actually deters visitors. Why doesn't the board do something different, and support our Museum of Berry Growing, newly opened thanks to the backing of the Berrydelicious Berry Farm?"

Cheers broke out. "Hear, hear! Claudette." Looking down at the floor, she saw woolen caps and hunting hats waving, including Clifford Junior's green-and-black check. Mr. Redsockett banged his gavel, then: "Ladies and gentleman, I call the question." The Selectboard unanimously endorsed Claudette's proposition, despite the fact that the Berrydelicious Berry Farm was now at war with the Museum of Berry Growing. (Berrydelicious employed organic farming practices. Their berry plants, along with the pesticide, fertilization, and harvesting methods, were certified 100 percent organic. However, the maple frames they used to keep the fruit from scraping the ground happened to have once been treated chemically to prevent wood rot. The museum, led by a gang of 'zero tolerance organic zealots' as the manager of Berrydelicious labeled them, advertised such frames as unacceptable.)

"Secret's out," acknowledged Harley. "You defied Euphoria. Yet you didn't touch her library. I don't see how you made the Shitlist." He tried not to notice either the moose eyeing his melted creemee, or the smell off the pond. It was growing chilly, and he dreamed of his evening bump of Old Grand-Dad by the fire.

"You will," said Claudette, folding into her red cashmere sweater. "Euphoria ruined the book collection. She pulped classics, for example *Tom Sawyer, The Mayor of Casterbridge,* all of Trollope's novels, saying they were not 'courtly.' She went after books containing 'Capital S-E-X,' beginning with the likes of *Tropic of Cancer* and *Lady Chatterley's Lover,* and on to contemporary 'steamers,' such as *Buster's Sugartime* and *Tango Makes Three,* replacing them with historical romances."

Harley seemed spellbound by this discourse. "I'm at sea," he muttered, while stroking his upper lip as if he had a moustache, which he once did, a small handlebar.

Claudette continued her recitation. "You know, an English heiress attends the country house ball and almost succumbs to the charms of the regimental captain—that sort of thing. Take Clare Darcy's Regency series, Barbara Metzger's trove led by *An Angel for the Earl*, Marion Chesney's debutantes and starving aristocrats—her trilogy of *Molly*, *Polly* and *Tilly*."

"I had no idea…" Harley trailed off. Sweat beads covered his furrowed forehead. "Why didn't the Library Board of Trustees intervene?"

"They did. At a closed session in April, I exposed this looting of literature, as well as her fake credential. Her library schooling consisted of a correspondence course from the University of Tawahus which, spelled backwards—'Suhawat'— sounds like 'So What.' I told them about her threatened boycott of the Book Nook, because they were selling the *Gossip Girl* series and 'other smut.' That swayed Francine Stutgart's in absentia vote: 'Something to dream about in the Fourway Corner Nursing Home,' she opined. Still, I worried a censure vote could go either way. That is when my uncle, Gaston Nadeau, intervened."

"Dear colleagues," said Gaston, standing to face the board. "Claudette came many times to my Fat Springs General Store with our mutual friend, Florenza, to have bowls of café au lait and bon-bons. I must relate a delicate secret. Florenza Fayette experienced the 'summer of love' in 1969 at Woodstock, just over our New York Border, with a man—Preston Penrose Rivers. They had met in the library, where P.P. was searching out magazines on motor repair—*Mechanics Illustrated, Popular Mechanics*. P.P. liked to tinker with his turquoise-and-white Chevy Impala and Florenza liked studying engines. After messing with the pistons, the carburetor, the gaskets, they sped off to Woodstock. They shared music and mud, but not each other. Florenza forgot it, but Euphoria did not. She and P.P. were almost engaged, and Euphoria could not let go of Florenza's 'wild ride,' as she called it. She and P.P. soon married, and they moved away." Gaston concluded: " At your service."

The board chair, Barton, tapped his Ticonderoga pencil on the tabletop. He flicked dandruff from his shoulders, his gesture before a call to order. Fixing a look on each member, arrayed as they were in a semi-circle not unlike the French National Assembly, he said: "Comments?" Silence spoke. "Hearing none, I call for a voice vote on the censure of Mrs. Euphoria Rivers. All in favor say *Aye*."

Claudette stared at Harley: "You didn't finish your creamee," she said.

"But I'll be able to finish my story about our town," said Harley. With that, he rose, then bowed slightly. "Thank you truly," he said, extending his hand.

Labette Luricoix's Favorite Color

David Rae

I am a necromancer. I've got certificates and everything. I saw an ad on Craig's List and sent them a text. I met this girl at the LaChute Community Center, and she was giving classes. Ten weeks to begin with, pay upfront.

What is a necromancer? Well, it's about communication. Communication is good, so the teacher said, honest and open communication. Open your heart, she told us.

It's good advice. I've opened my heart, and now I'm one hundred per cent open and honest. So let me tell you a little about myself, I'm twenty-four, blonde, people tell me I'm pretty. I work as a school district administrator. I've had a couple of promotions, and I got re-banded on the pay scale after the big merger with Vesuviusville School District. Guys: yes, I've been on a few dates, still have not met anyone special, but I'm hopeful.

Back to Necromancy. It's about communication. It's about talking. Some people have difficulty with that, and, dead people have a bigger problem than most. That is where necromancers come in. I know it sounds cool, but we're just like communication facilitators, except for dead people. We help people connect. That's what Valletta, the teacher, says.

The first class, everyone introduced themselves. Most of them were seniors, but there was one guy about my age, Preston Rivers the Third. He says most people call him Three-Pee, like in Star Wars.

Valletta told us anyone can do necromancy. You just need patience and a little faith. That's what we worked on for our first week. We spent a whole class just working on faith. It was funny. Three-Pee, kept saying, "I do believe in fairies." That's from *Peter Pan*. But if you don't believe the dead are alive then how can you talk to them? That was week one; chanting "I believe the dead live and will rise again." After two hours of that, not counting the coffee break, you really do believe the dead could rise.

Valletta told us that we should try and believe on our own during the week, the more we practiced at home, the more we would get out of the course. So first week's homework: chanting for at least half an hour a day. Do it either when you get up before work, or before going to bed, suggested Valletta.

The next thing we needed to learn was to contact dead people. Valletta had a skull to help us. We turned the lights down and lit some candles to create the mood. We only had one skull so we all had to take turns. I didn't want to touch it at first, but it felt cold and smooth. It's surprising just how heavy bones are. Soon I was really into it. So much so that I stayed in class during the coffee break. Valletta said that showed I was keen.

"You only get out what you put in," she told the whole class. "If you all work as hard as Labette you'll do ok. And don't forget there's a final assessment."

I was way ahead of most people at the class. Certainly, I was ahead of Three-Pee. He kept moving the skull's jaw up and down and going, "Yak-yak-yak." Valletta told him it was a necromancy class, not a ventriloquist class. I think Valletta was annoyed that Three-Pee wasn't taking it seriously. She kept taking the skull from him and saying, "Give someone else a turn," and "You know Preston, there are other classes on." But Preston III said he knew that already. His Grandmother ran her adults and seniors dance classes there.

He was dropping her off as her car was in the shop yet again and he had to wait. It was either Necromancy, or going to The Tipsey Towhee across the street. Preston said if he'd wanted to hang about with middle-aged drunks, he'd have stayed at home.

Once you have a connection with the dead person, it's real easy to talk to them. You focus on what you want to ask, and then focus on the answer. I asked the skull what its favorite color was and I got the answer. It was black, by the way. That seems to be most of the dead's favorite color. Some of them like purple as well, that's popular and so is crimson. My favorite color is black; it used to be yellow, but not now. None of the others in the class got an answer from the skull. Except Three-Pee, he said the skull told him that in the afterlife everyone is gay.

The whole class except Valletta laughed. Three-Pee is such a kidder and kind of cute, too.

Valletta told me I'd done very well. She was impressed at how easily I'd taken to Necromancy, and she suggested I might want to take the advanced class after I finished the foundation course. I said that I probably would. She told me it would still be at the community center. Foundation only really shows you how to speak to the dead. The advanced class teaches you to get them to do things like haunt people or move things or tell you hidden secrets, like where missing wills are.

"The dead do have their secrets," said Valletta.

Then we talked about where I could buy my own skull. They are quite expensive, and of course, plastic ones are no good. She suggested I might want to visit a graveyard at night and try digging up my own, or you can get really good ones from China on the internet. But make sure it's real. Once one of her students bought one online and it turned out to be a doll's skull.

Three-Pee was hanging about after class that day. He usually did. His grandmother was always late coming out of her dance class and that pink Dodge was always in the shop. I decided to go up and talk to him because, well did I mention he was cute. And funny.

"Hi," I said.

And he said hi back and grinned. I wasn't sure, but I thought he liked me. He's about my age and a bit of a geek. I didn't think he had a girlfriend because he was a bit scruffy, and not in a cool way, unless you thought tux-tees are cool.

Okay, he's not that cute, but he's my age and funny.

Okay, more annoying than funny, but he's my age. There aren't many young people here, and I don't get asked out on dates much, at least not by people my own age. Not that this was a date.

We were standing outside in the parking lot beside his electric, bright-red Kia Soul when I asked him, "You want to get a drink?" I know I shouldn't have, but you know a girl can't wait around.

"I can't," Preston said. "I have to wait for Grandma. I have to drive her home, her Dodge is in the shop."

"Okay," I said. I won't deny I was disappointed.

"But," he said, "I could meet you another time."

I didn't need to be asked twice.

So we are not dating but we've been out for dinner a couple of times, just at the IHOP. But it was nice. Three-Pee has started getting to the class early and sitting beside me when we do our satanic rituals. They're not really satanic rituals anyway, they're more about nature and the universe. Satanism is so misunderstood. That's what Valletta says.

Turns out, I didn't need to order a skull on Amazon. There was one in the department. When Florenza Fayette, the old chief librarian, died, she left her body to science. Sadly, science wasn't that interested in an octogenarian woman who choked on a fishing lure. They had, however, flensed her skull and returned it to the municipal office as per the terms of her will. The skull was supposed to sit on the new chief librarian's desk as some kind of reminder of the importance of keeping up Mrs Fayette's standards, but Mrs Euphoria Rivers had downright refused to allow it. Unhygienic, she said. That's why the skull ended up in a box in the stationary cupboard.

Me and Three-Pee started the ritual and raised old Mrs Fayette from the dead. Well, was she mad! She was not at all happy with the changes Mrs Rivers had made at the Library. I wrote everything down and sent it to Mrs Rivers in a letter. Mrs Fayette was particularly upset about Mrs Rivers throwing out all the back issues of *The Quonsettville Quacker* dating back to 1836.

"She is unworthy to be the guardian of our heritage," said Mrs Fayette and made me write that down in the letter. Apparently, Mrs Fayette's restless spirit now attends all the library finance committee meetings and glares balefully at Three-Pee's grandma who refuses to accept her motion to dismiss the chief librarian.

"Libraries are for people, not just books," says Mrs Rivers.

That's why I had to get a new skull and that's where you come in. Now let me ask you a few questions. Let's start with a nice easy one. What is your favorite color? Mine is black.

That One

Chuka Susan Chesney

Euphoria nearly shattered two glasses when she screen doored in at the Tipsy Towhee where I bartend Wednesdays and Fridays. She likes to unwind after teaching her dance class 'Twinges in the Hinges' for arthritic seniors at LaChute Community Center. I was anticipating her at the hostess station. She was a supercell of rage.

She kept sliding glasses toward me – I shrieked, told her I'm holding a paper umbrella and will flick olives at you if you don't leave me alone.

She leaned over the bar and whispered, "Darlene, I caught your little niece Hazel in my bedroom this morning, underneath my four poster! She sneaked in through the mudroom, was *ogling* me while I put on my …" and she mouthed the word *'panties'!*

So that's where Hazel has been taking her breakfast sausage every morning! To feed Euphoria's damn dog!

Mr. Harvey, the mailman, whipped around to help me when he heard – he'd shot the whole thing with his cell, said I stood up for myself by shrieking like a dying rabbit.

But Euphoria Rivers kept right on yakking, just like she was Queen of the May – strolled right past me after spinning a goblet round at the farthest stool, waited for me to stem on by, thinking I'd be bubbly enough to do that so she could tipple me over, and Harvey stayed nearby at the register till she left like the last bowl of peanut shells.

I was chipped – she was wearing the lemon twist blouse I had donated to the Community Center thrift store, plus her golden retriever bitch Clover bit me this morning when I reached over the fence to pick blueberries. I think that dog is a wolf-hybrid, and I don't think she's ever been spayed.

I said, "Euphoria, this is April 2nd. Did you ever get a license for Clover? I need proof she doesn't have rabies!" I held up my bandaged hand.

I could feel Euphoria's breath wanting to snifter me for standing up for myself as she tried to bowl me over when she kamikazied out the cowbelled door.

Descartes

Vickie J. Litten

Portia had her hand extended over the counter, holding the change from Mrs. Chatelaine's late fee payment, when she saw the front door of the library open, and Professor Braggadocio amble in. She dropped the coins into Mrs. Chatelaine's outstretched palm, and grasped the edge of the desk to pull herself up. She leaned her substantial girth forward, onto the counter, to peer at him.

The Professor noticed her scrutinizing stare. He tipped his brown tweed hat in her direction, then turned and was swallowed up by the aisles of books, tapping his silver-tipped cane on the floor with every second step he took.

Portia hefted herself up, and walked over to the open office door. Leaning on the door jamb, she studied the older woman with the thick silver-gray hair, bent over paperwork on the desk. "Mrs. Rivers," she said grinning, "the professor is here."

Mrs. Rivers looked up from her paperwork. "I don't suppose you could take care of him today?"

"Nope, you know he won't talk to me," Portia said. "He'll never forgive me for laughing when he was telling you that story about how he pollinated the stigma of his orchid." She shrugged. "Sorry."

"I would be more likely to believe you if you wiped the grin off your face."

Portia covered her mouth with her pudgy hand, and snickered.

"Very well." Mrs. Rivers put down her pen, and squeezed past Portia to get to the front desk. "Where is he?"

"He's still getting books. Oh wait, here he comes now." Portia plopped back onto her chair and gave a push with her feet, rolling it backwards, away from the counter.

Professor Braggadocio stepped up to the counter, dropped four large books onto it, and then straightened the jacket of his chestnut tweed suit. A short man, he had to look up to address Mrs. Rivers. "Hello Euphoria, you are looking well today."

"I see you in here every week. I look the same, Hubris. How are your orchids doing?"

"Wonderful." He smiled, "I have a pink cattleya in bloom."

She picked up the first book to scan it. "Nietszche," she said.

"I have decided to do some light reading in the philosophy field."

"Hubris," Mrs. Rivers said, as she scanned the next book. "Kant, Nietszche, Sartre and Hume are not light reading. More like concrete blocks. The only one you're missing is Descartes."

"I don't like Descartes. I completely disagree with him," he stated, throwing his shoulders back, and reaching up to finger his silver white goatee.

Mrs. Rivers looked down at the books, and sighed. "I do like Descartes," she said.

"You probably do not understand him," nodded Professor Braggadocio.

A red flush could be seen creeping up Mrs. River's chest and neck. "Hubris, why would you say that?"

"I may be retired, but I am still a professor. I know what I'm talking about."

"And I don't?" The flush deepened in color. "I also have a master's degree."

"Yes, but dear Euphoria, it is only a librarian's master. It's not a real master's degree." He stretched himself as tall as possible. "Not like mine."

From her vantage point in the chair, Portia cupped her hand over her mouth and whispered, "Remember, don't engage. Don't engage."

Mrs. Rivers looked at her, and scowled. "Too late."

"For one thing, Euphoria, you must understand," he waved his hand in the air. "Descartes' theory is simply intangible."

Mrs. Rivers shook her head, as if trying to toss something off. "Hubris, do you know what intangible means? All theories are intangible, by their very definition."

He frowned, "Well, then, you agree. I'm right."

"What? No!"

"And then, there is the matter of him changing his famous quote. I believe he changed 'I think, therefore I am', to 'I regard with compassion, therefore I am'. Even he didn't believe in his own work."

She cocked her head to one side and grimaced. "I think those are two different quotes, from two different books."

"Euphoria, I can see you are not sure of yourself."

Mrs. Rivers shook her head from side to side. "I don't have time to prove you wrong today, Hubris."

He smiled at her. "Indeed. In other words, you can't verify your statement."

Portia whispered, "Don't engage, don't engage."

"In my opinion," said the Professor, tilting his chin upward as he spoke, "Descartes was spouting propaganda to try and keep the common people civil, in a time of upheaval. You see, during the time of Descartes, France was transitioning from the Renaissance Era to the Revolution."

"What!" Mrs. Rivers, flung up her hands. "Hubris, the revolution didn't happen for over one hundred years after he was dead. It couldn't have influenced him!"

She rested her elbows on the counter, and buried her face in her hands. "Every week, I swear I'm not going to argue with you."

"Better you than me," laughed Portia.

"We're not arguing," said Professor Braggadocio. "I'm enlightening you."

"He is a professor," giggled Portia. "Maybe you should listen to him."

Mrs. Rivers tilted her head in Portia's direction, and mouthed the words, *Maybe next time, it will be your turn to be enlightened.*

Portia shook her head furiously, from side to side.

Mrs. Rivers gathered up the four books, and set them on the counter next to Professor Braggadocio. "Here you go, Hubris."

"Thank you." He reached for the books, then paused. "Euphoria, I was ..."

"Are you going to the Tea Room today, Hubris?"

He nodded. "Of course I am. I believe I will try blend number 35 today. It has just a hint of almonds and roses. I'm sure you would enjoy it."

"I will have to try it, next time I stop in. But right now I have to get back to work, Hubris."

"Of course." He picked up the books, and grunted under the weight. "Thank you, Euphoria. I will see you next week. I look forward to another stimulating conversation."

Portia giggled, "He said stimulating."

Mrs. Rivers admonished her with a quick glance. Looking down, she shuffled papers and straightened leaflets on the counter. "Goodbye, Hubris. Enjoy your books," she said.

They watched as he made his way out of the library, his body tilted slightly to one side, by the heavy books in his arm, his cane tapping on the ground, with every other step.

"That man will drive me crazy," said Mrs. Rivers in a low voice.

Portia wheeled her chair back up to the counter. "You wouldn't be the first," she said.

An Inconvenient Reminder

Howard Brown

We don't get much in the way of titillating news from around here; the usual boring, small-town stuff: births, deaths, engagements, weddings, total rainfall for the month of May… But the *shitlist* has changed all that: the letter Mrs. Rivers, the town's chief librarian, sent to Harley Pontchartrain, editor of the local paper, naming all the people who'd made her life such a living hell she'd decided to quit her job and move elsewhere. Everybody's talking about it.

Now our paper's not exactly *The New York Times*. Still, it's not *The National Enquirer* either and Harley wasn't about to publish the names of the alleged miscreants. But Bernice, office manager at our local paper, our local yenta and a blister on the ass of humanity who also just happens to be Harley's wife, had no such qualms; she made copies of the list and passed them out to everybody who'd been named, and emailed them to a few more. Harley was thoroughly pissed, but there wasn't a whole lot he could do about it after the fact.

So, while it's no secret who's on the list, nobody knows exactly what any of them did to get there, because the list doesn't say. Well, I guess the people on the list know, only they're not talking. But I know the story of one of them—Dexter Nail.

But who am I to be pointing fingers? Well, I'm not going to say. Dexter found out I was telling tales on him, who knows what he'd do? He gets riled, he can be a very nasty fellow. Let's just say that although I currently live in Quonsettville, I'm not from here. No, I'm a Southern boy, which is why I don't speak with that high-pitched, nasal twang like most everybody else in Vermont. But enough about me—I've probably said too much already—let's talk about our boy Dexter.

His family's supposed to have been around since the town was founded. And although I understand the original Nails were of somewhat common stock, they gradually worked their way up in the world, so that the last few generations have been considered local gentry. Dexter's granddaddy was a State Senator, daddy's a doctor, uncle's the City Judge.

Yet Dexter seems to be something of a throwback, gradually working his way back down the social ladder. At one time he apparently wanted to become a chef, attended New England Culinary Institute in Montpelier, I believe, but dropped out after a year and went in the Navy, from which he was discharged in short order; then came back home, picking up odd jobs here and there, yard work, rough carpentry, racking balls at The Angry Squirrel Pool Room down on Marvelline Road, that sort of thing. Just enough to get by. His main endeavor seems to be some book he's been working on for God knows how long. And that book, at least indirectly, is how he came to be at odds with Mrs. Rivers.

My job (and I won't say what that is either) gives me a lot of free time in the afternoon, which I spend at the public library, reading. And I hadn't been patronizing the place long before I noticed this guy who occupied the same table in back every single day. I didn't ask, but kept my ears open, and eventually learned his name was Dexter Nail.

Dexter's a disheveled little man, with a solid sleeve of tattoos running up his left arm and frizzy, blond dreadlocks that resemble nothing so much as a rat's nest. Year-round, he dresses in black jeans (ripped at the knees), t-shirt, leather jacket and Doc Martens.

He had books stacked four and five deep all over his table, little yellow slips of paper marking his place in each of them. I sidled over once when he'd stepped outside for a smoke and checked out some of the titles: *Beelzebub's Tales to His Grandson*, by G.I Gurdjieff; *Helter Skelter*, by Vincent Bugliosi; *The Seven Story Mountain*, by Thomas Merton; *Pilgrims of the Wild*, by Grey Owl; *Memories, Dreams, Reflections*, by Carl Jung; *The Late, Great Planet Earth*, by Hal Lindsey, just to name a few. I walked away scratching my head, unable to see the connection between any of them. Nor could I dispel the somewhat fetid odor which seemed to linger about the table.

But there he sat in their midst, like a spider on its web, periodically consulting one or another of the volumes, then pecking away furiously at a little portable laptop. This went on for some months and though Mrs. Rivers would walk back and speak to him from time to time, often loud enough that you could detect (even from a distance) a growing sense of irritation in her voice, the table remained in an utter state of confusion.

Then one afternoon the space had been cleared. No books, no laptop, nothing except the shining, blond surface of the once-cluttered oak table, now indistinguishable from all those around it. Dexter arrived moments later and stared blankly at the empty table, then looked about as if he were lost. What followed was a stream of profanities which turned every head in the room.

"What the hell have you done, bitch?" Dexter shouted, gesticulating as Mrs. Rivers approached.

"I did what I've been asking you to do for over a year, young man," she replied. "I've cleaned up your mess. And you need to lower your voice and watch your language. Otherwise, I'll have no alternative but to call the police."

"Bring 'em on, you flaming cunt!" Dexter screamed and Mrs. Rivers retreated across the room, fast making for her office. Dexter was right behind her, but a step too late as she slammed the door in his face. The walls of that office are glass, and we watched as she picked up the desk phone and began punching in numbers, while Dexter pounded on the door and continued to rant.

A few moments later, a siren began to sound somewhere in the distance.

Dexter tussled briefly with the two officers who responded, but was eventually cuffed and perp-walked out of the building. I watched from a front window as they stuffed him in the back of their patrol car where, legs churning, he began kicking at the windows, then the metal screen which separated the front and back seats.

Mrs. Rivers remained in her office until one of the policemen finally came back inside. The two of them spoke briefly, then we watched as she went back in her office, shut the door, sat down at her desk and, head in hands, began to sob.

Dexter was jailed, but released on bail later that evening. His hearing was held in City Court the next morning, which seemed awfully quick to me, but was apparently what his attorney requested. And I was right there, seated in the front row of the Courtroom.

After brief testimony, the Judge (Dexter's uncle) gratuitously declared that this appeared to be nothing more than an unfortunate misunderstanding and, as such, the charges would be dismissed, provided Dexter immediately tender an appropriate apology to Mrs. Rivers and she, in turn, indicate to the Court that the matter was resolved to her satisfaction.

It looked as if Dexter was about to skate, until he stood, turned to Mrs. Rivers and, with a razor-wire smirk, hissed, "Sorry, about the *unfortunate misunderstanding*, bitch."

His attorney was instantly on his feet, but before he could say anything the Judge motioned for him to sit back down.

And when the Judge spoke, his earlier, conciliatory tone had disappeared. "Mr. Nail," he growled, "I find you guilty of disturbing the peace and resisting arrest, sentence you to five days in jail on those charges and revoke your library privileges indefinitely. Further, I find you guilty of contempt of Court, for which you will serve an additional two days of confinement." Then, slamming his gavel against the podium, he added, "Court is adjourned."

Dexter was released a week later and by the following morning, someone had spray painted in large, red letters, "Mrs. Rivers is a flaming cunt," on the sidewalk in front of the library. There's never been any doubt as to who the culprit was. But proving those charges was another matter altogether (especially with a denial of culpability by Dexter) and no further action was taken.

City Maintenance did try to erase the words from the sidewalk, first with paint thinner, then with bleach, but a pale-pink version of the slur was still visible. So, they finally covered over it with a thick coat of black paint. And while this dark rectangle does obliterate the outrageous epithet, unfortunately it also serves as an inconvenient reminder to anyone entering or leaving the library of the egregious message which lies beneath.

There are lots of other names on the list, yet I feel Dexter's little caper is probably what pushed Mrs. Rivers over the edge. Still, given the boundless capacity of plain, ordinary people for abject cruelty, who can really say?

Estelle Burgstaller's Letter

G. P. Gottlieb

Francine Stutgart
The Fourway Corner Pines Center for Nursing and Care
27 McGibbon Street
Fourway Corner, VT 05480

May 16, 2019

Dear Francine,

I'm so sorry you've been unwell and hope you will be able to come home soon (also hope the people at The Pines are nicer than some of the reviews imply). We all missed you at our end of year Mahjong dinner (Virginia brought her usual rubbery cookies). Speaking of Virginia, she said (after she had that unfortunate breakdown) that The Pines serves delicious, fresh-baked rolls with butter. I hope that's some consolation for having been forced to be there. I don't know what I'd do if I had children and they sent me to a facility (really a nursing home) just because of a few minor falls.

Francine, I'm writing today to tell you exactly what happened on Saturday. It was after the dance recital in the Quonsettville Middle School auditorium. You've probably heard all about it (from Virginia and the other Mahjong girls), but I wanted to tell you my side of the story.

I was, as you know, the accompanist. You know I don't claim to be perfect, but it was absolutely humiliating to hear Euphoria Rivers publicly criticizing me in front of everyone. I had no idea why someone with her limited understanding of the arts would have the nerve to admonish someone like me who was trained in piano at the highly respected Castleton State College music program. If only you'd been permitted to go to college, Francine, you'd have loved Castleton. And there are probably several old Vermonters there who still remember one or two of my piano recitals.

Anyway, I know you're going to argue that Euphoria knows something about music because she ran that dance school in Burlington. Let me assure you that hiring teachers and taking parents' tuition payments, or whatever she did there, does not automatically qualify one as an artist of some sort. And she might know enough about dance to teach seniors a couple of times a week at the community center, but how hard is it to ask women to soften their arms and lift their torsos? It's not like she ever performed with the New York City Ballet!

My piano teacher, as you know, was our town's beloved Mrs. Jasna Djavanuken. She accompanied that august troupe during the reign of the great George Balanchine (her great granddaughter performed in Saturday's recital!), and I think she would turn over in her grave if she suspected that I'd been speeding through the Chopin Waltz in C# minor. I thought I would fall off the piano bench when Euphoria said, "I'm going to ask Mrs. Burgstaller to begin again at a slower tempo." She'd only been to one rehearsal!

Can you imagine my shock, Francine? The words "*Tempo Giusto*" are written on the music – did she think that meant it should be played as a dirge? I assure you that I was playing that waltz correctly at the most appropriate and universally accepted 'joyful' tempo. And does Euphoria have a degree in piano? No, she does not. Does she know anything about music whatsoever? Highly doubtful. And does anyone remember how much time and effort I put into accompanying those rehearsals when I could have been adding students to my schedule?

And yet, as you probably heard from everyone, Euphoria Rivers hissed at me and I had to start that waltz over. Nobody was upset with her for asking me to start again. All they remember is my response. All I said, in a polite, quiet tone of voice, was something to the effect of, "I think I know how to play a Chopin waltz." Pretty innocuous, I think, but next thing I know, Euphoria is telling everyone that I called her "a bitch." Maybe I said I had an itch, who knows? She said I whispered the word and that the dancers heard it. Well, what if I did?

Does anyone in this town ever say a bad word about Euphoria? You were there when she read that horrible nonsense at the February Poetry Appreciation Society meeting. You saw how everyone looked sideways and started fidgeting in their seats so that it sounded like a sudden rustle of wind blew through the library. You and Virginia covered your faces with your hands and the other Mahjong girls studied their nails, but I was trying to listen to her. And it wasn't my fault that she was bandying about words like "moist" and "thrust." So what if I laughed a teeny-tiny bit? Maybe I was thinking about something amusing. Did she have to make such a big deal about it in front of everyone? And I managed to read "Shall I Compare thee to a Summer's Day" without calling names or embarrassing anyone.

I excel at poetry recitation because my pronunciation, unlike Euphoria's, is precise. Mrs. Djavanuken used to demand very precise vowels from her piano students and said she couldn't understand children until they'd repeated the sentence: "Pack the black plastic bag," ten times, slowly and with no diphthongs, before each lesson. And in terms of quality, well, there is poetry and then there is poetry. I hardly think Euphoria's recitation of some modern nonsense about sexual congress is on the same level as a Shakespeare sonnet!

So, this is all to say that there was already some bad feeling between the two of us, and I think all rational-thinking people would say that I was justified in my reaction after the recital, when she told all the little pink-clad dancers and their parents that I'd probably rushed because I was nervous, that I was getting on in years, and that I'd never taught dance or knew what it was like to dance on a stage. Can you imagine? Why should I have taught dance? Everyone knows that I was always a pianist. And Euphoria is at least a year older than me! Getting on in years?

I'm not saying I'm perfect, but in the past few weeks, because of Euphoria, two of the mothers (of the little pink-clad recital girls) rushed their carts past me at the grocery and another mother pretended to be intrigued by the cauliflower selection. I'm just sick about the whole thing.

Even after how she spoke to me in front of the dancers and their parents, I apologized to Euphoria, because that is how I was raised, unlike some people who think everything they do is perfect. Did you know that Euphoria did not apologize to me? Not for singling me out during her poetry recitation, not for hissing at me to start over during the recital and not for implying afterwards that I had never been on the stage and that I'm too dotty to know how to play a Chopin Waltz at the proper tempo.

Really, Francine, I'm sorry for going on about Euphoria. Aside from that kerfuffle, everything here is fine and I'm reading a delightful mystery about a woman who accidentally stumbles over a dead body that turns out to be the local librarian (hee hee hee). But listen, please promise to not repeat a word of this letter to anyone. Maybe burn it. Some people in this town are terrible gossips, as you know.

Best wishes for a full and complete recovery!

Your friend and neighbor,
Estelle Burgstaller

Fish for Mrs. Rivers

William Butler

Euphratia's Tale

"I told Euphoria not to ever allow patrons to bring their grandchildren or children under a certain age to dance class. Not ever! But did she listen? Never! As hardheaded as always, and I would know. As her older sister, I can tell you she was as stubborn when given an ultimatum as if she were locked in mortal combat for her soul!"

"But Euphratia, it was amusing, was it not, I mean the entire episode?"

"Perhaps to you, Emily, but to Euphoria it was not anything but a declaration of war. By the way, what do you know of the entire circumstance?"

"I admit I've only heard differing stories, so what did exactly take place to earn both Dayman de Malville, and his mother, Taylor, Euphoria's enmity and place of dishonor on her, well, her (*whispering*) shitlist?"

"Quite simply enough, then, it started with Taylor, Mrs. de Malville, attending the senior's dance class, 'Twinges in the Hinges'... I know, but Euphoria thought it to be a clever name."

Twinges in the Hinges

"You will be going with me today, Dayman, I cannot leave you here by yourself for two hours while I am at dance class!"

"I'm 13! I can take care of myself and you know it! I am not going back to that damn class!"

"Watch your language and do not disrespect me, or you'll find yourself marching with me to every dance class until you're old enough to move out of this house!" and with that Mrs. Taylor de Malville and Dayman continued their familial warfare that morning until Mrs. Malville, Dayman in tow, began the trek from Bloater Hill to the LaChute Community Center, the towering, hulking son leading, shamefaced, eyes downcast, followed by his mother, proudly, eyes raised and smiling at each fellow Quonsettvillean who passed in person or passed by vehicle.

West on Marvelline Road, State Route 179, past the diner, the IHOP, the Angry Squirrel Pool Room, and it was there that Dayman, hailed from the open doorway by his chums, Barly Treppedo, and his twin brother, Marly, began his revolution.

"Mama!" he wailed, "lookit them, they gonna tell every kid in 6th grade I'm going to dance class!"

Taylor paid no mind to his wheedling tone although the hooting and hollering followed them past the gas station, even as they turned north onto LaChute Street and trudged past the library, dance class leader Euphoria Rivers' home base. Dayman glared left as they moved past that edifice, hating the brick building, and particularly hating the librarian not so much for her position but for this affront to his masculinity with a dance class for old women!

His anger built even as the squat brick building housing WQUO 103.7 FM and its "Good Times" music format came into view, was not quenched by he and his mother crossing the bridge over untroubled McCribben Creek, the last barrier before crossing the street and entering the LaChute Community Center, two nondescript quonset-type buildings, erected in 1948 and joined together in 1950. He balked slightly at the open doorway but was urged, pushed, by Mrs. Malville into the linoleum-floored space, music already blaring and where single women, seniors all, swayed. It was there he began plotting for his revenge against such indignity, although he knew not that word.

Later, the silent walk back allowed him to review his plot with glee, barely concealed from his mother. By the time they arrived back at their double wide trailer, he was ecstatic.

Revenge

Early the next day, a Thursday, Dayman met with his close friends, the twin Treppedo brothers, explained the plot to much laughter, and gave each his specific part, the timetable, the logistics.

Promptly at 5AM the very next morning, a quiet Friday, they met behind the community center, shook hands laughing the while, and set forth on their errands. Barly walked toward Quonsett Pond, hoping to find a lone fisherman with a stringer of bone-filled carp.

Marly hurried south to the Home-Away-From-Home Trailer Park where he found two empty burlap bags used for fertilizing the impeccable grounds, while Dayman lounged at the Angry Squirrel Pool Room, open everyday, 5AM til close. At precisely 6:30 AM he walked quickly, looking over his shoulder now and again, toward the community center, around the back where his two henchmen squatted. Barly had five nice-sized fish, not cleaned or gutted, and these were stuffed into the doubled fertilizer bags, then Dayman forced the rear door open to the community center and deposited the bags under a draped table. The community center was air conditioned, and the outside temperature was already a warm 75 degrees, a beautiful June morning. Dayman unplugged the conditioning unit from its outside receptacle, the gang then leaving as quickly as they could, heading off in different directions. The boys were sure that by the Tuesday afternoon dance class, things would be ripe.

Aftermath

And so it was. The first arrival on the fateful Tuesday evening senior group, Mrs. Hawthorne Peddly, wife of the retired judge, Herman Peddly, was overcome by the odor of rotted fish and left, nauseated, immediately. Her exit wasn't noticed since she generally opened the Center for the others. Four of the women, parking their vehicles, milled about the outside just as Euphoria parked her pink Dodge Dart and swept towards the closed doors. Turning to the assembled matrons, she announced, "Again, let us count our health as our blessing, and the leisure of dance as our reward!" And dramatically threw open the double doors of the Center.

The smell brought Euphoria to heel, she stumbled slightly into the hot, humid room, fell onto her knees, supplicant to the spoiled fish fully ripened. Other women leaned in, regarded the odor, and fled. None could find the strength to assist Euphoria back to her feet and out of the Center, but finally (probably not more than a full minute) she rose, and stumbled backwards in a move reminiscent of a merengue step, and with tears in her eyes, freely flowing down her face, her nose running with snail trails of mucus, she unsteadily walked to her car, fleeing to her home.

Her friends' and class members' telephone calls went unanswered for several days. Then on the following Saturday, Mrs. Renetta LaMare, widow of the late banker, Theodore LaMare, spread the word that Euphoria had investigated the odd circumstances of rotted fish hidden in the community center. Alerting the janitor, Chuck Hard, to the smell, she then

65

received the report from him of his discovery of the fish (which he unthinkingly reported as "strong as shit!" to Euphoria). His cooperation was sought and eagerly given since he was the one who had to clean the center, to rent huge fans to mitigate the smell, fumigate the place, and report the entire process, and cost, to the Board of Directors of the center. This was no easily dismissed chore, and one he was not competent to do nor comfortable with its completion … but he did so.

In other words, he was angry, very! He first visited the Angry Squirrel Pool Room, leaving word of the crime, then over to the Irving gas station where he received an eyewitness report from Larry, the special needs attendant of unusual activity along the road that fateful Thursday morning.

Then, finally, along the Pond's waterfront. It was there he found a grizzled, tanned, fragrant character seated on a plastic crate, hand-rolled cigarette dangling from his bewhiskered mouth, watching two cane fishing pole bobbers stationary in the tepid shallow Pond water. After explaining his mission, the old man said, "Well yup, there was a sneaky feller come by here 'bout a week ago, wantin' some fish, didn't care what kind, so I sold 'em some carp, yup."

Hurrying back to the center, now cleared of most of the smell, Chuck telephoned Euphoria with the news. From there she put the word out to all her students. Within an hour she received the reply she had so eagerly awaited. Pressuring her husband, Tully, owner of the Angry Squirrel, Mrs. Conquetta Rapshire, reported that her husband had overheard two youths, brothers, discussing the episode, implicating Dayman de Malville. Euphoria alerted the Quonsettville police department, and two cops were sent to the de Malville trailer where they confronted the mastermind. He (with his mother's support) refused to admit his guilt, thus ending the investigation since the others involved were also mum.

The Shitlist

"Dayman de Malville's name is on that list, followed closely by his mother's name, Mrs. Taylor de Malville. Do you see now, Emily, why? It is as it should be, and I am damned proud of Euphoria for calling out the names. At least those two. Of course, if she had merely listened to my advice this would never have happened. Still, it is funny, isn't it?"

Rank Frank

Claudia Bierschenk

In ihren Lungen wohnt ein Ahaaaaal
Auf meiner Stirn ein Muttermahaaal ...[†]

Whatever those lyrics meant (he had looked them up before but forgot again) – how he wished he was like Rammstein's music sounded! Strong, unshaken, manly. Age had taken most of his physical strength. But the anger was still there, his closest, most trusted ally.

Frank heaved himself out of the driver's seat, expecting the familiar flash of pain from his lower back all the way down to his toes, but it didn't come, not yet. Small favors. One last cigarette in the driveway and a quick wipe down of his black beauty. Oh, the smooth touch of the shiny exterior! Needs a proper shine first thing at daylight tomorrow. Tonight, it was the soccer match on TV and a six-pack of Pabst waiting in the fridge. Aaah, that first ice-cold sip slipping down his throat!

Frank looked over at the neighboring garden, the shadowy outlines of fruit trees, berry bushes, and flowers in the dim moonlight. She did have a green thumb the old cow, you had to give her that much.

Frank's *garden* was a barren landscape in this neighborhood. He didn't even have to cut the grass; the sun had burnt every blade of green to a faded, lifeless carpet of dead vegetation. The ramshackle house he was renting looked no better. Paint was peeling off the exterior like sunburnt skin. It stood out like a sore thumb among the neat family homes in the street. Parks Realty were probably chewing their pencils in anticipation of him leaving so they could bring in the bulldozer.

A grin pulled at the corners of his mouth. *Rank Frank you're such a bad boy!* Growing like weeds on her side of the fence, and, in fact through the fence onto his property – okay, his rental! Those flowers needed special watering. He unzipped his fly as he approached the fence and listened to his piss pearling off the chrysanthemum leaves. There was something so satisfying about that sound! But this was taking too damn long. Maybe he should get that prostate checked if he wanted to live his dream of leaving this shithole upon retirement, where he couldn't even make full use of the seven speakers he had lined up on his shelf. Only two more years.

Next door, the porch light flickered. Damn, they'd seen him drive up. The stupid cow herself lurking behind the curtains or her puppet of a husband. Nah, they'd probably heard the Rammstein's bass as he was driving up. But Rammstein had to be turned up loud, very, very loud. A tiny, unmanly gasp escaped Frank's throat as a figure stepped outside the door of the neighbor's house and just stood there, in the semi-dark, but clearly looking in his direction. His urine flow stopped, but he could feel he wasn't finished. Come on, get it out, damn those droplets!

"You need to get that prostate checked, Mr. Hauser!"

"Go fuck yourself!"

"Oh, aren't you just a walking cliché!!"

The screen door slammed shut, like a slap in his face. Okay, she'd caught him this time. Her idiot husband was probably walking that stupid dog of theirs. *Mr Hauser this, Mr. Hauser that.* Everyone else called him Frank. The guys at the Angry Squirrel called him *Rank Frank.* He was okay with that.

The old hag thought she was better than anyone else, more educated, more cultured, what with her dancing and being the chief librarian. All high and mighty ever since she came back from wherever she had run off to centuries ago. Didn't *he* have a rough job? Up at dawn, back by the time it was dark, all for the shitty pay on construction sites! You couldn't build things with books, could you? And now he was *assigned* to the playground project. Now that was humiliating! The guys at the Squirrel were already talking about it. *Building see-saws for the littles ones, Rank Frank?*

He gave his once-upon-a-time best friend a good shake and dragged his feet back down the driveway to collect his mail. No belated birthday card from his son. No surprises there. The usual bulk of junk mail, bills, and, hang on – a letter from *Parks Realty LLC*.

The taco meal deal from El Desperado's stirred in Frank's guts and an acidy air bubble worked its way up his throat. A letter from them was hardly good news. He burped, dropped the last of his cigarette, hobbled back up the driveway, tearing at the envelope. His porchlight flickered nervously, probably the sensor again. Frank scanned over the letter's small typeface keywords hitting him: complaint / loud music / urinating / house rules / neighborly peace / second warning. Heat rose up in his cheeks, his ears, spreading to his forehead, tingling the roots of his remaining hair. *Chubby fingers holding up a piece of scrap paper with something doodled on it. Couldn't draw for shit that boy. Can't I watch the damn game without you shoving crap in my face? Slap. Tears. Whining. Sorry, Daddy.*

*

Of course she had complained. Who else! Forever nagging to the agent because of the loud music! All the other neighbors minded their own damn business. Bam, bam, bam, his fist on her screen door. *Bam, bam, bam in her smug face!* Of course she didn't open it, probably on the phone to the cops already. Was she standing behind the door clasping her hands, holding her breath? He could hear the TV or the radio or whatever on inside. He shouted through the screen door, spraying droplets of spit on the fine mesh:

"So my music is too loud? Too loud? I have a hard job, I can play my music like I wanna!!!"

He gasped, nearly losing his balance on the step, as the door flew open.

His guts stirred a second time, more insistent, and he clenched his buttocks. This wasn't a good time for a fart. She stood there, in a ridiculously checkered bathrobe, as if wearing a chessboard. Reading glasses on her nose. *Smash, bang, his fist on her nose, glass splinters on the floor, blood.* What was she holding there? A brick to hit him in the head?

"I thought you might use this, judging from your taste of music, Mr Hauser."

She dropped what looked like a brick in front of him and slammed the door shut.

Just as he bent down to examine what it was – a German-English dictionary – a drawn out, flat sound escaped his anus, like the air out of a sad balloon.

† In her lungs there dwells an eel/there's a birthmark on my face

A Dream of More Cultured Days

Sally-Anne Macomber

"That woman left town as soon as she could catch a bus out," the witch had told me over the library's front desk, "without a backward glance or a hint of regret."

And then, "No one even remembers Sweets Crippen or her movies!" she'd jibed when she spied me rifling through the pewter bridesmaid gowns at Amber Black Bridal Boutique. "And she certainly had no time for this town."

And then, when I stopped to chat when she was lunching alone at the Notre-Dame Tea Room (and I'm sure, secretly reading a romance novel hidden behind a copy of *Vermont Fresh: A Fruit and Vegetable Handbook)*, Euphoria Rivers had said, "Miss Crippen wasn't born in Quonsettville, she was only *raised* in Quonsettville. She was born in Fat Springs. And Fat Springs wasn't part of the Greater Quonsettville Census area until 1953, some three decades after Miss Crippen was born. You must get your facts straight."

Chomping down on another Seconal, "My facts *are* straight," I'd said. "In fact," I'd enunciated as I watched her gray head settle back into her book, "Sweets Crippen was one of the greatest stars of the silver screen, and her autobiography was published by the Vermont Women Pioneers' Book of the Month Club, no less!"

And then I added, wiping cakey Seconal residue from the corner of my mouth because she hadn't the decency to offer me water from the jug she'd ordered with her rutabaga on rye, "The opportunity you are missing is ripe and golden."

Oh, it was so simple!

Nor did she have to do a lick of the work herself!

"The idea has three elements," I later said one evening as she stood pumping gas into her faded champagne pink Dodge Dart.

"I am not engaging with you on this matter again, Miss Nebulouse," she said, shaking the last drops into her gas tank.

"It's *Ms* Nebulouse, not *Miss*. And I am not hearing you, Mrs Rivers," I answered, stepping between the bowser and her car. "Because it is too important a cultural event to let petty small-town small-mindedness drive a stake through its heart."

She turned her head away and looked down Lapierre Street. "I have communicated all I have to say."

I stepped around her so she had to face me again. "I am saving you from yourself."

"I am on my way home from a busy day at the library," she said, turning back the other way. She replaced the nozzle on the bowser, screwed the gas cap closed, and snapped the fuel door shut. "Please step aside so I may pay for the gas I have put in my car."

I called out to her as she disappeared inside to pay for her gas. "I am saving you from a lifetime of cultural regret!"

"No one cares to remember old movie stars like Sweets Crippen," she said as she handed her VISA card to Sanjeev, the only Indian from India in Quonsettville and the only Indian from India to manage an Irving gas station in town. "You are harassing me, Miss Nebulouse."

"Harassment is my only recourse, Mrs Rivers. You refuse to return my telephone calls, you never respond to my emails and you have cancelled my library membership."

"Could you call the state troopers, Mr Gupta?" she asked, eyes wide and a tremor in her voice.

I raised my hands above my head in mock surrender. "Suit yourself then, I'm leaving," I said, "but you are killing the very hand that could be feeding this town."

"And," I shouted when we were back outside, just as she slammed the Dodge Dart's driver's door with her inside it, "The very hand that could be *saving* this town and your job and your family!"

Tonight 7.30pm, the paper on the noticeboard said. *Quonsettville Historical Preservation League meeting here.*

The LaChute Community Center, two old Quonset huts joined together, serves its community well.

Early by design, I stood just inside the front entrance. On the far side of the hall, Euphoria set out chairs in a circle, metal legs scraping on the linoleum floor.

I twisted the lock shut.

She looked up.

"No no no no no," she wailed.

"Hear me out, Mrs Rivers." I smiled as I waved a large roll of white paper in the air.

She stood stock-still as my shoes scuffed on the linoleum.

"There are only three elements," I cajoled.

She clasped her hands over her ears.

"The first is erect a huge screen in front of the library so we can hold the Sweets Crippen Film Festival. The screen would be so big we would need to close the whole building for six weeks in order to screen each one of Sweets Crippen's fifty-five movies."

She shook her head from side to side, hands grinding into her ears.

"That's one every evening, plus matinees on Saturday and Sunday. The festival will open with *I Was a Female Test Pilot* and close with *Stepping Stones to Moscow*."

She started mumbling. Though I was now on the other side of the circle of chairs, I couldn't hear what she was saying. And spit glistened on her chin.

"The second element is the Sweets Crippen Museum, to be established in the library's Reading Room. Quonsettville will swell with thousands of international visitors, and the library will get thousands of new members. Within five years, it's estimated the Sweets Crippen Film Festival and Museum will earn enough money to build a completely new library."

I dropped the roll of paper onto the chair in front of me. She opened her eyes and glared at the chair in horror. Then her body began twitching and her teeth began to chatter.

"That's the third element," I said, smiling down at the unfurled paper. "Removing that tacky statue of town founder Théophile LaChute from in front of the library and replacing it with a 100ft crowd-funded statue of Sweets Crippen. I've had the plans drawn up already. "

(My blood boils when I remember her response.)

"It's all so *very* easy and all so *beautifully* doable," I added. I stood to attention behind the chair.

(I have to wipe the sweat dripping from my forehead when I think about it, and swallow another Seconal.)

Looking directly at Euphoria Rivers, "You, Mrs Rivers, will be remembered as the woman who chose to memorialise Sweets Crippen, international film favorite and Quonsettville's most famous daughter," I said. "After all, only the truly memorable deserve a statue in Quonsettville."

Euphoria Rivers' twitching and shaking came to a shuddering halt. Her mouth clamped shut, she dropped her hands from her ears, and she lifted her head. Then she set her shoulders back.

"Miss Nebulouse?" she said.

"Ms," I said.

"Ms Nebulouse?"

I nodded.

"Ms Ninette Nebulouse?" she asked.

"Yes," I replied.

"Sweets Crippen may deserve to be remembered," she said, "and every town may deserve its own homegrown internationally famous film favorite."

Euphoria Rivers stuck out her chin.

"But Quonsettville has as its founding father Théophile LaChute, and over my dead body will a statue of my forebear be torn down and *replaced* by some *trampy actress*."

A waft of burnt toast floated under my nostrils.

Trampy actress?

Pain seared inside my chest as my eyes whirred. Clutching my twirling head, I watched spots of blood splatter from my nose onto the unfurled Sweets Crippen statue plans.

"I have my cellphone out of my pocketbook and I'm about to call the state troopers," she said.

The Sweets Crippen statue plans scrunched as my hand swooped down and swiped them from the chair.

Somehow I unlocked the hall door, and somehow I staggered outside, statue plans crumpled under my nose to stem the blood flow.

On the other side of the door, angry *Quonsettville Historical Preservation League* members stamped their feet and glared at me.

"Locked out by Euphoria's new gal pal," one jeered.

I would have made that sneering idiot eat his words but my head was reeling and with my spare hand clutching at air and grabbing nothing, I lurched towards my car.

Or what I thought was my car. As my body throbbed like it was being attacked by wave after flocking wave of vengeful eastern towhees, the bloodied statue plans slipped from my hand and slopped onto the hood of a Dodge Dart.

Nose still dripping, lungs heaving, chest sobbing at the *insane* desire of that *witch* to keep Quonsettville in the Dark Ages, I smeared the soggy mess of bloodied paper back and forth, back and forth, back and forth across the faded champagne pink paintwork.

And I would have left my revenge there except I had to drive home and plan the bombing of that tacky statue of Théophile LaChute.

Error of Judgment

Jane Andrews

Henry Devereux stared dreamily at Euphoria Rivers as she ticked him off in the register for 'Twinges in the Hinges'. Ah, Euphoria! – her name perfectly summed up how he felt whenever he looked at her. She was the only reason he attended this dance class – without his eagle-eyed wife who would have been all too quick to notice that Henry always raised his hand when Euphoria asked for a volunteer to help her demonstrate the next set of dance steps. Mind you, there was only one other gentleman in the class – and Barney had recently had a hip replacement and wouldn't be doing anything strenuous for the next few months.

Euphoria wasn't like the rest of Quonsettville's 'senior' population: for one thing, she was a lady – always properly attired, no matter what the occasion; and, more importantly, she had an intellectual nature, as he did.

Briefly, he allowed himself the luxury of remembering the first time he saw her, when he was a young and idealistic English teacher at Quonsettville High. It was his first teaching job – at twenty-one, he was only three years older than Euphoria – and he'd been blown away by the intelligent mind of this girl who'd just transferred from St Everine Catholic Girls' Academy. Although initially quite conservative in her dress and appearance (long hair in a tight ponytail and unflattering spectacles), she'd suddenly blossomed into a bright and vivacious young woman who blurred his perception of the teacher/pupil relationship. He often wondered whether, had he told her of his unrequited love, she would have become Mrs Devereux instead of Mrs Rivers. Ironic, really, that now she was the teacher and he the student.

At the end of the class, instead of leaving with everyone else, Henry hung back to talk to Euphoria. "Excuse me," he said politely, waving a leaflet at her, "I was wondering if you'd seen this?"

'This' was a flyer advertising a lecture in Fourway Corner the following Saturday evening.

Euphoria glanced at the flyer, then shot Henry one of her rare smiles. "F. Scott Fitzgerald!" she said excitedly. "He's been my favorite writer ever since I was in high school!"

"I know," Henry confessed shyly. "I taught you in your senior year." (He'd never mentioned this before.)

Euphoria's eyes widened in surprise. She'd thought the name Devereux was familiar but hadn't connected Henry with her high school English teacher, assuming him to be much older – an uncle, maybe. "Of course!" she exclaimed. "Henry Devereux! I remember you teaching us about Hemingway. You were young and handsome – we were all half in love with you."

Henry decided to ignore her use of the past tense.

"I was thinking of going," he said casually, "and I wondered if you'd like to accompany me?"

(He would tell his wife, Violet, that he was going with a male friend. She hated literature, so she would be pleased he hadn't asked her to accompany him.)

Euphoria smiled warmly. "I would love to," she said simply. "My husband isn't much of a reader. It will be lovely to spend an evening with a cultured man."

*

Henry dressed with care on Saturday evening, knotting his tie with trembling fingers as he imagined Euphoria removing it later. He'd always suspected she was attracted to him – there was something about the way she'd looked at him when they'd demonstrated the tango a few weeks ago. He closed his eyes, picturing himself running his fingers through her short, gray hair as he pulled her towards him in a passionate clinch ... and then his mind faltered. Where could they consummate their desire? he wondered. He had courted Violet by taking her to the Notre-Dame Tea Room – back then it had been called something else. What was it? Ah, yes, The Hungry Chipmunk – but Euphoria deserved something more sophisticated than a cup of camomile and a cream cake. (Although it would be admittedly erotic to watch her push a whole chocolate éclair into her mouth in one go.) Was there a hotel in Fourway Corner; or would they be reduced to making out in the back of her car, like teenagers? It still rankled that his own car was currently being repaired at Bill's Garage and that Euphoria would have to give him a ride.

It was 6:30 when Euphoria's old, faded, champagne pink Dodge pulled up on Shakespeare Street. She'd already told him that her 'proper' car was currently on loan to one of her grandsons, but he thought this one somehow suited her more: the color was more ... ladylike.

Henry called goodbye to Violet and hurried out of the house. He didn't want his wife to see the car and start becoming suspicious. Opening the passenger door, he was confronted with a large handbag on the seat. "Just pop it in the back," Euphoria told him, busily reapplying her lipstick. (He took it as a positive sign that she wanted her lips to look enticing.) He did as he was told, noticing as he did so something that looked suspiciously like Georgette Heyer's *The Spanish Bride* lurking in Euphoria's bag. Surreptitiously pushing the volume to one side, his eyes took in another three by the same author, confirming his suspicions that Euphoria was indeed a passionate woman. Perhaps later they could re-enact some of Heyer's racier scenes!

The drive to Fourway Corner was a pleasant one. They briefly discussed each of Fitzgerald's novels and then moved onto his short stories. "You don't know what a pleasure it is," Henry said truthfully, "for me to talk to a woman who likes books."

Euphoria laughed. "I'd be a pretty poor librarian if I didn't! Anyway," she sounded suddenly wistful, "I can't share my love of reading with my husband – all he ever seems to do is watch TV crime shows and sports."

Henry heard the unspoken hint in her words. She was obviously giving him the green light to go ahead later.

Despite looking forward to this lecture for weeks, Henry couldn't concentrate on anything the speaker said, all too aware of the intoxicating presence of the woman at his side. Even her perfume gave off a muskily suggestive scent; and her splendid bosom strained at her blouse as if begging to be released. *Soon, my darling, soon,* he thought absently, in his mind already kissing her mouth, her neck, her shoulders. The talk passed in a blur as he indulged in a very happy fantasy that involved himself, Euphoria and the back of her car.

"Do you have time to sample the refreshments?" he asked her tentatively as the lecture finished and people began rising from their chairs.

Euphoria swivelled her gaze in the direction of the supper table. "Well," she began, in what sounded to him like an incredibly flirtatious tone, "I wouldn't mind a cup of tea, but what I'm really interested in are those wonderful éclairs."

Henry almost choked on his excitement as she pushed it into her mouth.

It was when they were once more seated in Euphoria's Dodge that Henry made his move. Before she could start the engine, he lunged at her, grabbing her startled face in his hands and attempting to plant a kiss on her unwilling lips. "Oh, Euphoria!" he moaned passionately, his lips moist with anticipation. "You don't know how long I've been waiting for this!"

"Mr Devereux!" she cried, scandalised. "I am a married woman!"

"I don't mind!" Henry protested.

"But I do!" She recoiled from him in horror. "And you, sir, are a married man!"

"Violet doesn't understand me." As a defence, it sounded impossibly weak. "She doesn't like books and she doesn't like sex," he elaborated. In fact, he'd been sleeping in the spare room for the past three years. "No one would have to know," he said, almost pleadingly. He felt suddenly old and defeated.

"*We* would know," she said quietly. "Mr Devereux, I'm sorry if I've given you the wrong impression, but I could never let anything develop with another woman's husband."

"It needn't be an affair." He sounded desperate now. "Just a one-off – that's all I'm asking for. If I could just kiss you once ..." His voice tailed off as he noticed her icy disapproval. She was staring straight ahead, not even thinking him worthy of eye contact.

"You're a sexual predator!" Disgust dripped from her words. "Your wife needs to know what you get up to when she's not around. How many other women have you lured into your clutches in this way? How many more innocent victims have been promised literature and then had to fight off wandering hands?"

"None!" he replied, shocked at the accusation. "You're the only one. I love you, Euphoria. You must know that." Then, as she reached into the back of the car for her handbag, he began to panic. "What are you doing?" he asked as she fished out her cell phone.

Her tone was icy with contempt. "Ringing Harlequin Pontchartrain. I think this is something for the *Quonsettville Quacker*, don't you? The whole town needs to be warned about you. Women need to know you are a man not to be trusted."

"No!" Henry surprised himself by grabbing the phone from her hand. How could he have misread the situation? She'd given him so many signals.

"You know that's not a solution." She sounded quiet, calm. "I can just drop by the *Quacker*'s office and tell Harley in person. After all, I drive past it every day on my way to and from the library." She paused. "I'm sure a story like this will make front page news."

"You won't say anything." For the second time that night, Henry surprised himself. "You won't say anything to anyone," he continued. "Not to Harley, not to my wife, not to your husband – because if you do, I'll tell everyone about the Georgette Heyer novels you hide in your handbag. What sort of librarian will you be then, if the whole town finds out you like trashy romance novels?"

The blood drained from Euphoria's face. "You wouldn't dare!"

"Try me," Henry said, his face calmer than Quonsett Pond at sunset.

Euphoria fastened her seatbelt and started the engine. The two pink spots in her cheeks only enhanced her features – features Henry now knew he would never touch again. He dug his nails into his palms. Cursing for not having waited longer, he consoled himself with the thought that Euphoria probably wouldn't have lived up to his expectations. Nevertheless, he could not ignore the uncomfortable, tight feeling in his pants.

Perhaps, he thought idly as Euphoria, shrouded in indignation like a cloak, drove them back to Quonsettville, he should try again in six months or so. He knew he would not be able to switch off years of infatuation in a matter of moments. If anything, the haunted look in her eyes made her even more desirable. At this moment, he thought dreamily, ignoring the tense silence that filled the car, she perfectly summed up his favorite Fitzgerald title: *The Beautiful and Damned*.

Justice is Served

Chris Hall

At school I was academically slightly above average and did particularly well in the dramatic arts, but languages baffled me silly. Regrettably, Vermonters take pride in their proficiency in French linguistics, so the practice and development of French-language skills is a scholastic imperative. Usually I choose not to fraternise with the academically minded, but when it serves my purpose, I make an exception.

It just so happens that an astute girl called Euphoria, new to the school, had a considerable aptitude for French. During our senior year at Quonsettville High, in fact, Euphoria won the French medal. So, I gladly exploited her knowledge for my benefit when I felt the need.

So one day during French class, the teacher decided to impose an impromptu oral exam. Each of us had to stand up front and briefly tell everyone what we did last night, in French.

The previous evening my mother had made jam, one of her culinary specialities, and I helped her. While I waited my turn, I took the opportunity to query Euphoria regarding the French word for jam. She whispered, "en français they call jams preserves, so just say *préservatif*."

That was all I needed, the rest I could manage. When my turn arrived, I marched up to the front of the class with self-assurance and announced, "hier j'ai fait des préservatifs, j'ai donné à ma mere à goûter." Which of course meant, "Yesterday I made jam, and I gave some to my mother to taste."

The class giggled. The teacher shook her head in disdain and asked me if I was having a laugh. I peered at Euphoria for validation. She nodded and winked back confirmation. No, I assured our educator, that is exactly what I meant and was immediately banished from the study group.

I was confused. After class, several pupils emerged to mock and malign me. Pointing fingers and sniggering. Once I caught up with Euphoria, I queried the ambiguity.

"Perhaps I ought to explain," Euphoria smirked, "that a préservatif is actually a condom in French."

Strike one!

Much like me, Euphoria was a tenacious, single-minded woman, which is why we initially got along rather well, but as they say, opposites attract, yet similarities repel, and after that incident, repel we did.

I think it was her rigid personality that eventually created the conflict. She was hellbent on her own self-aggrandised success; her facetious onslaughts toward me were unparalleled.

Euphoria was smart, I'll give her that. Nevertheless, from now on, no more solidarité with Euphoria the she-devil. A purulent animosity grew between us like a malignant tumor. At least it did for me; how Euphoria felt about it, I'll never know.

Anyway, I get ahead of myself. Introductions may be prudent. My name is Bambi Chaste. I'm a woman of style and taste. Quonsettville-born and -raised.

From a very young age I became aware that I instinctively emanated an innate allure. I can't explain it, that's just the way nature created me. Flawless genetics I suppose.

My long blonde hair and curvy physique launched me into prominence just as puberty arrived, and they've served me well ever since.

My mother always told me, as a woman your brain will only get you so far, be prepared to use the other assets god gave you to propel yourself to success. Know who you are and you will win your battles. But remember, if you choose to fight, first count the cost, and always believe in yourself.

Once I accepted my own potential, I began to cultivate it as a senior at Quonsettville High and refined my infamy within this quaint little town as head cheerleader.

That is where my notoriety began and my popularity within the football fraternity became unrivalled. The girls wanted to be me, and the boys just wanted me.

Qu'ils mangent de la brioche, in other words, let them eat cake, as I was not prepared to fraternise with le proletariat.

I was however, prepared to fraternise with the beau monde. That meant formulating a collusion with the St. Everine Catholic Girls Academy to raise my communal prominence and secure a candidacy in the inaugural Miss Quonsettville beauty contest, which resulted in my crowning as Miss Quonsettville.

If I was honest, Euphoria's academic achievement awards had bruised my ego, so securing the beauty contest was my consolation. However, I don't believe in harbouring grudges, I give credit where credit is due.

Although, vanity can be very cruel if you don't know how to manage it, but vanity is my favorite sin and sometimes I need to fall back on my genetics to nurture it.

A short time later I read in the *Quonsettville Quacker* that Euphoria Dubonnet had married in St. Balthazar's Episcopal Church and was now Mrs Preston Penrose Rivers. There was a picture of the smiling couple! Strange, I didn't receive an invitation to the wedding. Perhaps it was lost in the mail.

It was many years before I heard of Euphoria again. I married a local teacher, Randy Chaste, who taught physical education at Quonsettville High and coached the school football team.

Then one day, out of the blue Randy told me Euphoria was back in town. Curiously, she hadn't made contact with me; you'd think she'd be over her petty jealousy after all this time. I would have gladly arranged a welcoming soirée with some of the old sorority sisterhood; in a gesture of fraternity with a genial gateau, or maybe a humble pie.

It seems Euphoria had studied for a Master's degree in library science at Tawahus University and had taken up a position as the Chief Librarian at the Quonsettville library.

A Master's degree no less, it seems her aspirations had merely brought her back to where she started. The higher you go, the farther you have to fall. The more you gain, the more you can lose.

I personally decided ambition was not the be all and end all. As Abraham Lincoln once said, "I would rather be a little nobody, than to be an evil somebody." There is something to be said about us underappreciated domestic homemakers who are devoted to engendering family values in pursuit of our genus. Without benevolent inhabitants like us around to pro-create, no one would exist.

Anyway, we moved in different circles, so for a long time I successfully avoided encountering our illustrious Chief Librarian, until one fine afternoon I popped into the Notre-Dame Tea Room for an undisturbed fortifying latte.

Time passed quickly while engrossed in *Death of a Librarian*, a book I picked up at Leaves of Lorraine Book Nook just the day before: I love murder mysteries. After about fifteen minutes, three women entered the café and sat a few tables away. I had my back to them, but I unquestionably recognised the voices. One of them undeniably my old nemesis, Euphoria. I hunkered down, determined not to be identified, circumspect, yet straining to hear every word with apparent nonchalant indifference.

They talked rather loud and excitedly, so I could easily hear everything they said. It was general chit chat, catching up on old times. These were former school friends indulging each other in some self-aggrandised mutual appreciation, enamored of Euphoria's idiosyncratic achievements.

The other two were sisters, Lilly and Marjorie, who were back in town after attending their uncle's funeral. Euphoria was tediously insipid with her consolatory platitudes, but once out of the way, they quickly returned to their sycophantic flattery.

One of them fallaciously beguiled Euphoria with, "Weren't you the very first Miss Quonsettville back in your heyday?"

"Indeed, I was!" came Euphoria's reply.

I immediately had to bite my lip to stop myself from screaming out, "You lying bitch, it was me!" With unimaginable restraint, I resisted. Frozen apoplectic, almost aspirating the last vestiges of my latte when it regurgitated into my throat, I contemplated my next move, before impulsively deciding I could stand her monstrous lies no longer. I slipped out of that café, concealing my wheeze as best I could, and made a dash back to the sanctuary of my bunker.

Strike two!

Back home, I collapsed onto the bed in an infuriated rage and stared at the reflection of my wrinkled face peering back at me from the dressing table mirror. The glistening tears merely enhanced the creases.

I walked to the wardrobe and pulled out the discolored white satin sash with faded yellow *Miss Quonsettville* depicted in lurid tacky lettering.

To know your enemy, you must become your enemy. Remain ignorant of them and it is certain to end in tears. Disarm them and wait for a moment they do not anticipate.

Next step. If your opponent is emotional, seek to irritate her. Pretend to be weak, so she may grow arrogant. Attack when she is unprepared, appear where you are least expected.

Euphoria assumed the worst was over, that's when I decided the time was right to shame her. I drafted a letter to the editor of the Quonsettville Quacker, Harley Pontchartrain, stating that the Chief Librarian is falsely claiming to be a former winner of the Miss Quonsettville beauty pageant.

Strike three and you're out!

A few weeks later, the paper published an exposé on significant events in Quonsettville's history. It made mention of the Miss Quonsettville contest, an institution now for so many years. To celebrate, they listed all previous winners of the title, going back to the first year's winner in 1969, Miss Bambi Biloxi, now Mrs Randy Chaste, proudly listed for all to see.

So, there it was, no mention of Euphoria. Local news is scarcely an upset for anyone who never bothers to take notice. Perhaps it prompts minor gossip to accompany a coffee first thing over the morning paper.

Nevertheless, a victory barely won is better than no victory at all.

Euphoria Rivers, la justice est servie.

Out-Shush the Librarian Challenge

Beatriz Seelaender

There's a certain pride in it. I like seeing my name on things. *Agatha Mignonette* – the youngest person on that list by a couple of months, as my best friend Taxie Molina was born in September.

I have, of course, been the youngest at a lot of things – from Spelling Bee state champion to, as the legend goes (according to my mom), having learned to read at age two. So, it is safe to say I am a regular at the library – at least I had been, until the events of The Other Day.

Ever since I can remember, I have always wanted my own nemesis – if I ever grow up to become an international super-villain, I will be sure to mention this "shitlist" in my acknowledgements: "last but also least, thank you to my very first enemy, Euphoria Rivers, who I ran out of town at the ripe age of twelve…"

Okay, I should not take all the credit for it. Everybody on that shit list is a hero. Taxie and I, of course, are sure to have been the main players, but everyone has done their part.

It started on a quiet Friday afternoon a couple of months ago, when Taxie and I were hanging out at the library reading through the works of the Serial Scribbler – someone had been vandalising the library books with permanent marker: mostly they made fun of the books, which frankly made them more enjoyable.

We were laughing at the scribbles on one book called *The Perks of Being a Wallflower* at which the scribbler seemed quite annoyed, and old Euphoria straight-up shushed us.

"There's no one else here!" Taxie said.

Euphoria simply pointed at the "*This is a place for reading: please be respectful of others*" sign that had probably been there for twenty years. At one point, someone else had made a sign that read: *Kindly Shut Up*, but that had been taken down within a week. Honestly, I would have respected the second sign a lot more.

"Do you think it's Dayman?" Taxie hypothesized. She has this ridiculous crush on Dayman de Malville, previously nicknamed Dayman de Smellville before he got popular and stopped hanging out with us.

"I don't think Dayman knows how to read."

Taxie blushed. She thinks she can conceal her crush so well.

"SSSHHHH," Euphoria said, and I think I saw some ungodly spit come out of her mouth.

"Again, there's no one else here!" I said.

"Why don't we go hang out at the drive through?" Taxie asked.

"Because that's where everyone else is?" I said as if she were stupid.

"But we can, like, talk and eat there…"

"SHSHSHSHSHSHSHSHSHSHSHSH!"

Now, that was hella impolite. So I reacted a bit harshly:

"SHSHSHSHSHSHSSHSHSHSHSHSHSHSHSHSHSH SH!" I said it back to her.

Taxie thought it was hilarious and, after finally containing her giggling, also said her piece.

"YEAH! SHSHSHSHSHSHSH YOU!"

We got banned from the library. It was awesome. If a teacher gave us an assignment to look something up, we would just say, "We can't, on account of us being banned from the library". This made us sound so much cooler and mysterious than we were – we had an adrenaline rush for five days.

Our hangout spot was upgraded to Leaves of Lorraine Book Nook, where we were allowed to speak. On the weekend, however, while we were silently reading books without paying for them, guess who showed up.

Euphoria and her husband, a few shelves ahead.

And oh, how loudly they spoke!

"I'm just saying, *Bones* and *Castle* are the same show," her husband was saying, just.

"I am not having this conversation with you again, dear. Perhaps instead of watching television you could read a book. How about Alice Munro's *Family Furnishings*?"

"No, if I'm going to read something, it will be a crime novel. I am retired, dear."

"What does that have to do with anything?"

"Shshshshshshshshshsh," Taxie and I started. They couldn't see us at first. She then saw us and crossed her arms, visibly perturbed but still trying to keep it together. We knew she had not told her husband about The Other Day, as he sounded puzzled:

"What's that about?" he asked, and we shushed him.

Our shushing was quiet at first, like a buzz only they could hear. Hopefully Euphoria wondered whether she was going crazy. As she got closer, our shushing became louder and more intense. She told her husband not to do anything about it; we weren't worth it (nice thing to say about kids, by the way).

They left the store after about fifteen minutes. By the time Euphoria and Mister Euphoria were leaving, our adrenaline rush was back: Taxie and I looked at each other, and suddenly knew exactly what to do.

We promptly followed them, shushing them all the way back to the library, where they had parked.

We'd been hoping one of them would flip. It didn't happen then, so we started keeping tabs on Euphoria. Whenever either one of us saw her, we would call the other and shush her away. Sometimes we would meet up in front of the library and shush her from afar, so she could see us through the window and know what to expect when she left work. I suspect she stayed back at work at least a couple of times in the hopes that we'd give up. One Sunday we followed her to church and back to the library where she usually parked her car. Someone walking with her – it must have been someone related to her, as she also had the same perpetual expression of discontent – asked about us, and Euphoria simply answered:

"I don't hear anything."

On the third week of us doing it, she finally flipped on us. It was a Saturday morning, and we had been waiting for her at the library.

We hadn't even been doing it for long, when she turned abruptly and completely unexpectedly. A large vein throbbed on her forehead – we now realized no one else was around. She could show us her true hair-nostrils-on-display-from-inflated-nostrils-due-to-anger self:

"SHUT THE FUCK UP! SHUT THE FUCK UP! SHUT THE FUCK UP!"

We were kind of shocked, as no old lady had ever said that to us. And she kept on saying it; she couldn't stop saying it, and that was all she said all those times.

You wonder if that's what she'd been keeping herself from saying whenever she said *Sshh*, as if it was just the beginning of that elegant sentence.

"Jeeez, Louise!" I said, "Calm down!"

Taxie was giggling. "Jeez, Louise," she was saying.

"Come on, let's go. She might kill us."

So we left the lady going mad on the sidewalk. I guess eventually she came back to her senses.

Euphoria Rivers has been officially defeated. After years of incessant shushing, she has been out-shushed.

That night, Taxie and I went to get burgers at the drive-through. We were thinking of ways we could spread the story so that our classmates would know about our great accomplishment without it looking like we were bragging, so we decided we would speak really loud and they could listen in. It didn't quite work out, though:

"Shshshshsh," they said. "Shshshshshshshshshshshshshsh."

With Euphoria gone, I guess we are going back to hanging out at the library.

On Rutabaga: Chester's Story

Christopher Muscato

Chester Manolo Franklin III knew why he was on the list. He didn't need a personalized letter from Euphoria Rivers, ink-stained with her tears, to explain it. Of course, he never received such a letter. He never received as much as a middle-finger salutation as Euphoria rode off into the sunset in her sputtering Dodge Dart. But still, he knew. It was the rutabaga.

What Chester didn't know was how many other people in town were aware of the circumstances behind his unfortunate inclusion on the damning list. And honestly, that thought was driving him mad. Chester looked himself in the mirror, clammy fingers straightening his suit jacket and fidgeting with his starched collar and tie. His snow-white hair, normally perfectly combed over the top of his balding head, had proven impossible to tame this morning. His forehead glistened, and he dabbed the perspiration with an old but stylish paisley handkerchief. With a deep exhale, Chester turned from his reflection and shambled out the door, so preoccupied he didn't catch the paisley handkerchief as it flitted from his breast pocket, snatched by the morning breeze.

All Chester noticed in that moment was a slight browning around the leaves of the hollyhocks lining his walkway. He felt a tinge of guilt at realizing they had been neglected these past few days. At 72 years old, Chester had never married or had children, but he had his beautiful Victorian home on Station Street, within walking distance of work, and he had his hollyhocks. There would be no Chester Manolo Franklin IV, and he was okay with that.

Chester looked at the house with its neatly painted shutters. His mother had once lived here too. He used to walk home from the office for lunch with her every day. She always cooked something he liked.

Chester's shoulders slumped as he turned from the house and faced the street. There would be no home-cooked lunch today. He had to face Quonsettville.

"Morning, Eva," Chester said, his voice tight as he strove (but failed) to exhibit his normal confident demeanor. "Medium latte, skim milk, please."

"Sure thing, Chester," Eva Martinez smiled reassuringly as she rang up the order. Chester's heart was pounding. What was that expression, that tone in her voice? What did the woman know?

As Eva set to work pressing espresso beans, Chester leaned against the counter, his thumbs twiddling as his eyes oh-so-casually surveyed the interior of Evita's Coffee. It was crowded that morning, full of patrons engaging in the ritual grinding of the gossip mill. Normally, that's what he loved about this place. Today, however, he would have preferred to grab coffee somewhere further from the library, but this was where he usually came on Tuesday mornings. He didn't want anyone thinking he was avoiding his usual routines. Out of the corner of his eye, Chester noticed Eleanor Duke and Violet Devereux suddenly lean over their drinks amid furious whispers. He was certain that Eleanor had looked directly at him a bare moment before.

"Here you go," said Eva as she set his drink on the counter. The sudden movement in his periphery made Chester jump.

"Yes, thank you," he mumbled, snatching the paper cup, pivoting towards the door with such haste he forgot to ask for a coffee sleeve.

As Chester arrived at work, his hands burning from the un-sleeved latte, all he could think about was rutabaga. The word haunted him. Ru ta ba ga. He shuffled into the municipal office, neck buried in his shoulders and polished Italian shoes quiet against the carpet. Nodding curtly to the secretaries while tucking his chin into his crisp collar, he was careful to avoid anything resembling a conversation. Rutabaga. Finally: Office of the City Planner. He'd made it. Chester felt an extraordinary sense of relief, a long, deflating exhale escaping his lungs as he scurried inside.

Of course, peace and solitude were not what this day had in mind for Chester.

"It was the Burgendoffer House, wasn't it?"

Startled, Chester looked up from his work to see the recreation manager from the Parks Department, Manny Esposito, leaning in his doorframe.

"I'm sorry, what?"

"The Burgendoffer House. That's why you made the list, right?" Manny plopped into the chair across from Chester's. "Everyone's talking about that damn list. Everyone. It's nuts. So, that's it, right?"

Chester's leg began to bounce under his desk.

"Yeah, could be …"

Manny nodded to himself, the corner of his mouth raised in satisfaction.

"Want to get lunch today? We could take some sandwiches from JJ's down to the ferry dock."

Chester simply nodded, his mouth too dry to speak.

"Ha, ducks," Manny chuckled as he tossed crumbs from his meatball grinder into the water. Chester quietly chewed his pastrami on rye, watching the ducks splash in the water.

"Gentlemen, pleasant afternoon."

Chester snapped his head around.

"Hey, Bill," waved Manny. "You see that Chester here made the Shitlist?"

"Sure did," Bill replied.

Chester gasped in surprise and swallowed a chunk of pastrami. It stuck in his windpipe, and covering his mouth with the back of his hand as he wheezed and sputtered, his face broke into red splotches. The ducks in the water watched on, hoping the rest of the pastrami sandwich would be tossed into the water.

"Easy there partner, don't need me calling the paramedics, do we?" Bill grinned, tucking his hands into the belt of his police uniform.

Doubled over, Chester waved off Bill's remark with the hand still clutching the offending sandwich, wiping his eyes with the other. With a few thumps of his fist against his chest he straightened up, red splotches still glowing.

"You know why he's on it, right?" Bill asked Manny. "He lost Euphoria's dog."

"You lost Clover?!" Manny exclaimed.

"Maple," Chester rolled his red eyes. "Dog before Clover. This was right after they moved back to town. Euphoria asked for a favor."

"And you lost her?"

"They got her back!" Chester protested.

"And an animal-at-large ticket. Had to go to the municipal court and everything," Bill chuckled. Chester grumbled under his breath, tossing the remainder of his pastrami sandwich to the ducks.

"Hey, I thought you said you were on the list because of the old Burgendoffer House."

Chester shrugged as he and Manny worked their way up LaChute Street and back into the office. His forehead burned hotter and hotter. He didn't need Manny digging too deep into this.

"I mean, she was pissed about that house," Manny continued. "I know it was decrepit but when you, the city planner, refused to endorse the Historical Preservation League's proposal to preserve the house … man, I thought she was going to burn down your office. And by proxy, mine. Hey Gloria, Joanne, did you know that Chester lost Euphoria's dog?"

"Clover?"

"No, Maple."

"Oh, I remember Maple."

Chester gasped again, inhaled some spittle and doubled over, coughing into one elbow and leaning the other against the secretary's desk.

How he wanted to grab Manny by the shoulder, spin him around and punch him in the face.

"Is that why you made the list, honey?" asked Joanne, unconcerned by the old man wheezing by her desk. "That was years ago, but people have long memories, I suppose."

"You mean it wasn't because of that time he got her community quilt sale cancelled?" Gloria mused, examining her nails.

"He did what?" Manny grinned, leaning on the desk and looking pointedly at Chester. Chester rubbed his forehead with his fingers.

"They didn't file the vendor forms to use the community center," Gloria explained, leaning over her desk and lowering her voice to a dramatic stage whisper. "So he made them cancel all events until they were in compliance."

"Chester made them cancel a quilt sale?"

"There was a bake sale he called off, too."

"Uh-huh. Now was this before or after he lost Maple?"

"After."

"But before the Burgendoffer House? Damn, man, how many times have you wronged this woman, Chester?" Manny grinned impishly at Chester.

"Oh, don't you know, honey?" Joanne exclaimed before Chester could interject a word in his own defense. "Chester and Euphoria have known each other practically their whole lives. Even when they were kids. Been through a lot together, right honey? In fact, I had guessed that you were on her list because of ... oh, never mind."

Chester's heart started pounding, threatening to beat its way straight through his double-breasted jacket. Beads of sweat sprung up on his brow. Was this it? Had Joanne known about the rutabaga, the thing far worse than anything else, the entire time? Did she know why Chester deserved his place on the list?

"Oh, all right, I can see you're all bursting to find out," Joanne said gleefully. "When they were kids, Chester and

Euphoria built a tree house and practically lived in it together … before he put up a no-girls-allowed sign and gave up her spot to Jacob Brown!"

"Oh, Chester, wow, that was cold," Manny whistled. "So that's why you made the Shitlist?"

"Yep, that's, that's got to be it." Chester nodded, his head bobbing up and down like a dog watching a tennis ball. His white hair, now thoroughly disheveled, revealed the bald spot he was always so careful to comb over. He rubbed the back of his neck, feeling the clammy sweat against his hand, his once crisply starched collar now soggy and damp. Manny lowered his chin to observe Chester.

"No, that's not it. Look at you, Chester. There's something you're not telling us. You know what it is, don't you? You know why you're on the list."

"Honey, don't push him. If he doesn't want to share, he doesn't –"

"No, it's time." Chester gulped. Rutabaga. Rutabaga. It reverberated in his head with every pounding heartbeat. Ru-ta ba-ga Ru-ta ba-ga. This was a weight he had carried with him for far too long. He needed to do this. Rutabaga. He needed to come clean. He took a slow, deep breath, looking out the window at the heavens before beginning his confession … but at that moment a flash of paisley danced through the air just outside the window. Chester's eyes bulged, he looked down at his breast pocket in a panic, and he bolted out the door.

Unforgivable Sins of a Possum Murderer

Jenna Hillhouse

Simon Hunt, or "Buddy", as everyone called him, spent his days walking the streets of Quonsettville looking at the ground. It started with finding a $20 bill once, then turned into picking up loose change, and had then since morphed into finding disregarded things he found interesting. He'd take his treasures home and place them in a china cabinet. The good stuff he placed proudly on the mantel next to his Purple Heart.

Buddy came home one evening with a box in his hands. His sister was busy in the kitchen cooking dinner when he walked in. She came over now and again to help with house chores, though he insisted he could do it himself.

"Welcome back," she said as she wiped her hands on her apron. "Dinner's almost ready if you're hungry."

Buddy placed the box on the counter.

"What's in the box?"

He smiled. "Open it and find out."

His sister narrowed her eyes with suspicion, but her curiosity always got the better of her. Buddy counted on that. She tipped the lid back, and within a second was crashing to the ground on her butt, her arms flailing.

"What the hell, Simon!" she screamed, grabbing the counter to pick herself up.

He laughed and reached into the box, picking up a small possum that was playing dead. "I found her today on my walk. Sweet lil thing, ain't she? Don't know how she got to these parts, but she made it, didn't you, Lady," he cooed, petting the now awake and alert marsupial.

That was how it started.

Buddy and Lady loved to prank the townsfolk, each day looking for their next "victim". Tully over at the Angry Squirrel Pool Room chased them out with a pool cue. Young master Dexter Nail dumped all the coffee in his Evita's Coffee cup onto his lap, yelling how he wasn't going to include them in the acknowledgments for his book. It was sure to be a bestseller.

The kids were always the funnest to tease. They'd scream and run away, but not a minute later, they'd be back at his side, asking if they could pet Lady, to which he'd oblige. Lady loved the attention. The best reaction was from Sanjeev at the gas station. He no sooner saw Lady, than he was throwing the "Take a penny, leave a penny" coins at them while hollering, "No, no! You don't bring that in here!" They racked up a whole 12 cents that day.

Their prank at the library took a little more planning, since they had to time it just right. Buddy found a beat-up hardback copy of one of the big Harry Potter books and hollowed it completely out. Lady scurried into the book and rolled up as tiny as she could before he closed her inside. The book drop was a tiny chute outside that led to a bin just behind the reference desk in the library. He lowered her gently into the book drop slide with some string just as Mrs. Rivers opened the collection bin. Buddy kept hidden to the side of the entrance, standing on his tiptoes to peer into one of the old windows that distorted his view.

Euphoria Rivers stacked the books onto her cart and wheeled it over to the front desk. One by one she opened the front covers and checked the due date slip (who still uses those?) before scanning the barcode to check it in. When she picked up the book with Lady in it, he felt a rush run through his spine. This was it!

Mrs. Rivers finally opened the false book and screamed when she saw small beady black eyes staring straight at her from inside a seemingly innocuous hardbound. She fell out of her chair in an effort to move away from the desk, and scrambled on her hands and knees over to the book repair station.

Buddy chortled and slapped his knee, wiping the tears from his eyes.

Euphoria Rivers scanned the area around her and found a yardstick resting near the tape and scissors. She began swatting at Lady, who was now in a panic and dodging the blows, all the while hissing at Euphoria. Lady somehow had sense enough to not play dead while the librarian swung wildly, but would stop to bare her pointed teeth between swings.

Buddy stopped laughing and rushed over to the library's entrance, which was still locked. He cupped his hands to the glass so that he could peer in, and watched as Mrs. Rivers screamed, "Get out! Get out! Get out!" while chasing the agitated Lady around the room. Buddy was just about to knock when he saw Lady jump for an open window at the back of the room. He rushed to the other side of the building, but after calling her name over and over again, she still did not return.

"You damn woman!" he said to Mrs. Rivers as she switched on the library's automatic doors. "How could you do that to my poor possum?"

Euphoria stood there, stunned. "That vermin was *yours*?! How was I supposed to know? It popped up out of nowhere!"

"Well, thanks to you, now I can't find her!" he said as he stomped out of the library. "This sucks."

News got around town about Buddy's missing possum friend. LOST posters began littering the telephone poles and store windows; a desperate plea to help reunite one of the town's three Navy veterans with his beloved pet – the thing that had given him the most joy after his wife's passing seven years ago. The *Quonsettville Quacker*'s editor, Harley Pontchartrain, came to interview Buddy and ran a column on the front page, offering a reward for Lady's return. For three days he looked high and low to no avail; and for three days, it was all anyone could talk about and speculate on.

One evening, a knock on the door roused Buddy from his chair. He opened the door to see PP, Euphoria's husband, with a solemn look on his face. "Hey, Buddy," he said. "I, uh ... I found Lady on the side of Nord, but ..." he trailed off. "I'm gonna tell Euphoria when I get home, so I'd appreciate if you didn't say anything to her yet."

"Oh," Buddy said, nodding. It had always been a possibility; people in town didn't exactly drive slow on Nord Street. "I guess I'll go collect her then," he said, his voice shaky.

"Why don't you have some friends come over, have a funeral for Lady. She deserves it."

Buddy nodded and walked out the door.

Only a couple phone calls and a mass email later, the backyard filled with the townsfolk who had come to adore Lady in the last couple of months. Even Euphoria Rivers came, though she stayed near the back of the crowd. Word got around how Lady came to be missing, and while everyone knew it to be an accident, there were still stares and whispers. Two of the most affluent town gossips, Bernice and Maggie, stole glances at her and clicked their tongues. *Beloved Possum of Navy Vet Killed by Local Librarian*, Maggie would later suggest to the newspaper. It would practically write itself!

"I heard she threw Lady out the window and watched as she ran into the street. She jus' didn't say nothing," Kyle, one of Barly Treppedo's friends said to him as he dug into his ear.

"*I* heard she knocked Lady out and PUT her on the road!" Barly said.

Marly Treppedo, brother and twin of Barly, nodded. "She prolly did kill Lady herself," he said, trying to ogle the dead possum.

"I heard she called her 'vermin' before kicking her 'cross the library," said JoJo, Marly's little unofficial girlfriend.

It was the biggest affair to have happened in the town for two years, ever since Chuck and Frank decided to cohabitate.

Buddy had finished digging the grave and setting Lady inside when he turned to everyone. "Thank you all for coming," he said between sniffles. "Lady would've appreciated it." It was all he could manage before he turned to start shoveling dirt back in. The residents took turns scowling back at Euphoria, who pressed against the wall of the house, looking at no one while tapping the side of a cup of tea.

It was a somber evening, complete with beer, a grill full of hamburgers and hot links, and cupcakes from the new vegan café, all donated by local businesses. Buddy shook hands with the residents offering their condolences and well-wishes. After people had their fill and most went home, Buddy found Euphoria, who stood two steps from the door.

"Look – uh. No hard feelings?" he asked, his eyes rimmed red.

She eyed him, and with a tight smile responded, "Sure. No hard feelings," before walking outside and shutting the door.

Neveah and Hunca Munca Visit the Library

Mary Krakow

Neveah opened each Beatrix Potter book to an illustrated page. She stood three open books on end forming six walls of a fort. The pages fanned inward making it too small for her pet mouse Hunca Munca who, still confined in the carry-all, scratched to get out.

"Hold on," Neveah crooned. "Let me fix your little house." She rummaged in her book bag and pulled out a fat pink eraser, a fidget spinner, and a hackey sack. She rearranged the books so the edge of one book held open the pages of the next. She used the eraser and the hackey sack to prop the pages open for a door. Beatrix Potter illustrations made giant murals on each wall. This would be perfect for Hunca Munca to play house. "There. Almost ready." She fished out a milk cap, tiptoed to the drinking fountain and filled it with water.

Hunca Munca squeaked.

"Okay, okay." Neveah put the water and fidget spinner in the middle of the fort before unlatching the carry-all. Then Hunca Munca made a beeline for the water and promptly tipped it over. "Wait here," she told the mouse.

Neveah rushed to the bathroom and pulled a dozen paper towels from the dispenser. When she returned, Hunca Munca's fort was empty. She mopped up the spilled water, then looked under the library table. "Hunca Munca!" she whispered. "Where are you?"

Hunca Munca did not enjoy her outings to the library. First of all, there was that stupid nineteenth century calico dress with a white apron Neveah dressed her in. Besides, the cold hard table hurt her delicate feet. And what was up with the giant mice on the walls of the house Neveah made for her? They were terrifying.

Her escape plan had been percolating for a while. The spilled milk cap was the distraction she needed. Hunca Munca scampered down the table leg the moment Neveah left for the bathroom. She scurried across the carpet and hid on the bottom shelf between Kevin Henkes' *Chrysanthemum* and *Lily's Purple Plastic Purse*. Now those mice had style.

Neveah crawled around on the floor and searched. "Hunca Munca. Hunca Munca, come here right now!" Neveah felt a presence towering over her.

"What in God's green earth are you doing on the floor?" Without waiting for an answer, the librarian continued, "Get up this instant."

"Yes, Ma'am." Neveah stood.

"You didn't bring that lizard back in here, did you?"

"No, Ma'am."

"What's all this then?" asked Euphoria, pointing at Hunca Munca's fort.

"I was just looking at—"

"—The library is no place for hackey sacks and fidget spinners."

"Yes, Ma'am."

"It's time you went home."

Neveah didn't dare disobey Miss Euphoria. She'd have to return tomorrow to collect Hunca Munca.

Letter To The Editor – About Angus

Gary Zenker

To The Editor:

It's a damn shame how so many people forced Euphoria Rivers to leave our lovely little hamlet. Maybe printing the entire name listing will help the people here think about how they treat others. Oh, if I'm not allowed to say 'damn' in this letter, just edit that out.

It's no surprise that Angus and Jasper Tipton were on the list, probably at the very bottom, with a star each for emphasis. They were constant thorns in Euphoria's backside, if you know what I mean.

It's not that Angus doesn't have some charm going for him … that smile, his very manly physique and his natural abilities in fixing near anything that runs on electricity makes him more popular than Pop's maple cheddar pancakes on Sunday, which as you know is quite an accomplishment and way better than anything at the IHOP on Marvelline Road. Why he didn't change the name of JJ's Sandwich Shack after buying the place five years ago, I don't really know.

It's natural to get a crush on a teacher or a librarian, especially one who is as educated as Euphoria Rivers. Thomas Kincaid's boy, Gerry, had a crush on Selma and Vic's daughter teaching Sunday school. But that was years ago and Gerry was only six. At 35, Angus could almost have his choice of the single women in town; he didn't need to make advances on Euphoria, a married woman. True, the health issues her poor husband had affected not only his ability to walk but also to perform a husband's duties behind closed doors, if you know what I mean – she's complained of it herself when she got tipsy at Korsakoff's a couple of years ago during her husband's 70th birthday party, so I'm not gossiping. And having the name P.P. – I'm not making fun – makes it both ironic and a bit embarrassing. But that doesn't make it right. Honestly, a handsome young man chasing a woman thirty plus years his senior is just uncomfortable for everyone.

Angus wasn't fooling anyone by leaving the gifts of flowers anonymously to Euphoria. And dear Lord, his constant questions in researching poisons that kill without leaving a trace in autopsies. We never read true crime or murders in our twice-monthly book club with Euphoria leading them and who has any business with that kind of thinking except someone who could get himself in a whole lot of trouble?

And as if that wasn't bad enough behavior, letting his St. Bernard Jasper roam free … we have leash and poop pick-up rules, even if our own, very rotund Police Chief Turpin turns a blind eye to anything that requires him to leave his office. Who uses a lazy-boy for a desk chair anyway? That wooly mammoth (Jasper, not the Chief) attacked Euphoria's cousin's Pomeranians Puck and Moth. Euphoria took over caring for the cuties after cousin Joy ran off with Ted Lambert, Jake's boy from his second marriage. Dumb as a post but she did win the county Maple Syrup Queen contest three years in a row.

Did you know that the pups were named after Shakespeare characters? I was over her house for tea one evening when we heard the poms scream and ran out to watch Jasper trot away with poor Puck in his mouth, leaving behind a pile of excrement that can only be described as ungodly large. The same thing happened a week later with Moth, making me wonder it might have been some kind of sick retribution for Euphoria's rejection of Angus. Her retriever Clover did nothing during the chaos, which I guess just goes to show that guests, even if they are dogs, should never outstay their welcome.

I'll admit it was mighty brave of Bernice, keeping Angus and Jasper on the list, given that he is her step-nephew – I mean Angus, not the dog who is obviously not your step-nephew. (Maybe you want to take that part out, too.) We all appreciate the fact that she knows that the truth is the truth and that the *Quacker* has never been afraid to handle the hard situations, like when your undercover reporter discovered that Rickard was at one time charging above-list price for used tractors or Dayman de Malville was responsible for a number of the missing bikes in our community. How he thought he could advertise them for sale in the *Quacker* and not get caught … well, let's just hope he becomes a baseball player or finds a trade that doesn't require common sense.

I only mention all of this because if Angus is still looking for someone, he should put an eye toward someone a little less encumbered and a little closer to his age, who could give him the attention he needs and about which I could make a suggestion or two.

Euphoria isn't (wasn't) the only educated older woman in this town. There are some with more free time and would be more appreciative of the attention of a virile young man with repair skills and earthen needs.

And the book club will continue to meet but I will now lead it at my home. Oh, and our next book will be 'Tale of Two Cities' and all are welcome to attend. I will begin leading the group this Friday night, assuming I can get all my lamps working correctly to provide adequate lighting.

We will put out home-made cookies for snacking.

Pets are very welcome.

Sincerely, Agnes Whitehead
Lifelong Quonsettville resident
Mother to Maisy and Daisy

Flight from Quonsettville

Holly Saiki

The Eastern Towhee I was carving from a White Spruce fell from my hands as I stood up. I dashed over to the couch, where Karen was sitting, a piece of white paper flapping in her hands.

"Where did you get the letter?" I said.

"Abby gave it to me at Lunch Recess."

"Really, let me see," I replied, leaning over my daughter's shoulder and grabbing it from her grasp. "Where did Abby get this?"

"From her Aunt Bernice. Your name's on the shitlist."

I knew about the shitlist. The whole town knew about Euphoria Rivers' shitlist.

"It's good to see all the money spent sending you to St. Everine Catholic Girls Academy isn't going to waste," I said, sitting down again.

I read the letter in all its sanctimonious glory. Euphoria Rivers' florid purple prose painted herself as a wounded martyr, driven away from the town she loved by the unprincipled monsters dwelling here. I bit my tongue, trying to prevent myself from laughing.

"Usually, when Euphoria wants to complain," I said, "she'll show up at a Legislative Breakfast or a Community Dinner to argue in her typical passive-aggressive manner when she doesn't get her way. But a letter to the editor is a new tactic. All I did was protest her library rule stating parents need to be with their children when they want to check out a book. It's not like I dramatically overturned her whole life."

I flipped the letter over and read through the names on the list on the back, my name, Dwayne Hoffell, located in the middle.

"You started the whole protest, Dad," Karen said. "You really stood up to the old bag."

My mind drifted back to the time of my noble strike against uptight prudery, leading a substantial army of seventy-five determined parents and excited, giggling kids toward the library. We walked with a grand purpose through the automatic sliding door, squeezing as many people through the door as possible, savoring the joy of rebelling against Euphoria's draconian rule. I looked directly at Euphoria as she was checking out a picture book for a mother with her young son. Euphoria glanced at us, her mouth a huge O of surprise, as if somebody had stomped on her prized flowers, staring at the large crowd spreading across the floor and milling around the reception desk like a herd of water buffalo. Euphoria stood up straight up like a ruler, shoulders back and plastering on a stiff, phony smile.

"Welcome to the Quonsettville Municipal Library," Euphoria said, her voice dripping frost as she glared at us, her head turning back and forth as she took in the crowd, "What does your group need help with?"

"Thank you, but we don't need any help at the moment," I said, giving her a smug grin. "We just want to see what books we want to check out."

"I see," she said, her eyes scrunching as she grinned, baring her pearly white teeth, "I hope the people in your little group enjoy themselves … quietly!"

"We will," I said. With a simple hand gesture from me, the group broke up, heading to several different library sections like silent homing missiles. Yours truly went to the adult fiction section, Karen walking behind me, as Euphoria glared at our retreating backs.

Karen and I were the last people to head to the checkout counter. A small pile of Stephen King books in my arms, I gently placed them on the counter.

"I highly doubt this is appropriate literature for a young girl," Euphoria snorted. She had bags under her eyes, her shoulders slumping in exhaustion dealing with such a large group of people during spring vacation.

"Don't worry," Karen said, placing her library card on the counter, "I've read R.L. Stine's 'Fear Street Series', Stephen King isn't any gorier than he is."

"But all of the adult subjects?" Euphoria replied, "I shudder to think what sort of effect Stephen King has on a young mind."

"Don't worry, I've had to read plenty of dark novels in my English class," Karen said, "I know not to let fiction warp me into a serial killer."

"And I'll make sure she doesn't reenact anything from Stephen King's stories," I replied, "Isn't it a *parent's* duty to monitor what their kids consume?"

Euphoria glowered at me, her cheeks a dark red and lips trembling. She checked out the books way too quickly, roughly passing each through the scanner and pounding the stamp on the first page. Then Euphoria shoved the books towards me with the tips of her fingers. I bit my lip.

"Thank you for visiting the Quonsettville Municipal Library," Euphoria said, "I hope you enjoy the books."

"I will," I said, giving her my cheeriest smile, "I hope you don't mind if our group returns tomorrow. There's always so much to do at the library, especially on Spring Vacation."

"Alright, fine, the rule is rescinded, are you happy now?" Euphoria said, hissing in my face. "Now get out before I call security."

A hand touched my shoulder, bringing me back to the present.

"Daddy," Karen said, "Do you think Euphoria has left for good?"

"I'm not sure," I replied, putting the letter down, "All I know for sure is a lot of people are going to be happy she's left Quonsettville."

"Well, I'm sure glad she's going," Karen said, her voice sure and steady, "I don't know why the Quonsettville Municipal Library hires old bags who shriek at the first mention of blood in a novel. Why can't we get a cool chief librarian?"

"I'm not sure myself," I said, smiling at her as I shook my head gently, "But they'll appoint a new one pretty soon. Hopefully, they won't be a nutcase like Euphoria was."

"I hope it'll be a hunky guy," she said, kissing me on the forehead. Karen took the letter and walked back up the stairs, a spring in her step. I gave one last glance at her before returning to the table to finish my White Spruce carving. All thoughts of Euphoria faded away as my knife bit into the wood.

Camp

Melisa Quigley

In some ways Travis feels more grown up than his sister, Caroline and his brother, Jarrod. It's not because Travis knows more things. He knows less and likes to observe people. Whenever he's asked for his opinion, he waits to see what his peers say before commenting. He believes Caroline thinks she knows everything because she's so opinionated. When she talks to Jarrod about his friends at school, Travis remains silent. He knows secrets they don't know. More important things.

He's in the Quonsettville Boy Scouts, in Raven District, which he's not happy about because they've decided to include girls and changed the name to BSA. There are twenty boys and the community refer to them as grubs who must be cleaned up afterwards because they're always getting themselves dirty. So far, no girls have joined and the club leader, Robert Green, decides to take the boys on a camp.

Travis's best buddy, Charlie Ticker, gives a comic salute before they march around the east side of the pond and set up camp with the other boys. Just up from the pond is Gunnarson's beach. The boys wash their laundry in the pond with soap. Herman Pedley, the retired judge, supervises, sitting on a rock smoking his pipe taking in the scenery when a wet singlet flies and lands beside him.

'Knock it off,' he says and throws the singlet over his head. Charlie catches it.

When they've finished, Robert and Herman lead them on a trail looking for different birds and terrain.

'Make sure you all have your cameras ready so you can take pictures along the way. Why who knows, you may even see some black bears,' says Robert and chuckles, knowing they won't. 'At least you'll have two more badges, okay.'

The boys don their backpacks and pair off following the leaders, excited about what they'll see and the prospect of having a Camp and a Photography Badge to add to their collection.

'I need to pee,' says Travis to Charlie, when he really needs to crap. 'I'll be back soon.'

He moves away so no one will see him and walks through the bushes and crouches down. The tall grass fronds tickle his buttocks and he glances around for something to wipe himself with before pulling up his shorts. He sees a flash of black and hears heavy breathing and murmuring. Curious, he cowers thinking it must be an animal.

The librarian, Euphoria Rivers, dressed in black shorts and a white blouse, is walking her dog Clover off-leash. It squats and to his disbelief Euphoria does too. Her frilly white panties sit around her ankles and Clover runs off in the opposite direction. Sweat glistens on Euphoria's milky white cleavage. Her eyes narrow and her nose scrunches and she grunts. He can't believe the loud noises she's making. She's always telling students in the Quonsettville Library to be quiet and behave themselves. He hurries to pull his camera out of his backpack, trying not to make any noise, and presses the zoom button. Euphoria remains still like an animal about to be shot … before glancing in his direction. He lies prone in the dirt in case she's seen him and pauses before snapping the photo, inching his body along behind a bush. His heart thunders in his head.

He snaps another one as she rises to pull up her panties. Clover runs towards him from behind as Euphoria calls out to her.

'Well, I never. Have you been spying on me, Travis Johnson?'

Travis throws the camera into his backpack and runs off to find Charlie and the other boys.

Her face turns scarlet and her voice raises an octave. 'Come back here or I'll report you to your club leader. I wasn't feeling well and wanted ...'

Charlie laughs when he sees Travis.

'You look like you've seen a bear.'

Travis turns around to reveal the lush trees surrounding the pond and breathes a sigh of relief.

After dinner, the boys talk around the campfire until the embers die before climbing into their sleeping bags under a starlit sky. Tomorrow they'll camp at the beach before returning home.

Travis waits until the other boys are asleep before showing Charlie the photos. They remove their sleeping bags and walk past Mr Peddly and Mr Green who are both snoring. Travis's torch lights their path. He searches for his handkerchief; he knows he left it there earlier that day.

When camp breaks up, Travis can't wait to go home. His duffel bag smells of sweat, wood smoke and yuckiness. Obtaining Camp and Photography Badges excites him, but now other things do too. Travis and Charlie decide to write Euphoria a letter and enclose what they've found. After school, they go to the library. They walk around the books and the office, making sure Euphoria isn't there before sitting at one of the vacant computer desks to type her a letter. Travis's hands falter over the keys, thinking she's going to come up behind him at any minute with the Principal and have him kicked out of school. He prints the letter and Charlie picks it up off the printer, while Travis deletes the file. At home, Travis cuts out letters from *The Quonsettville Quacker* to form the words *guess who* and pastes them at the end of the letter.

Euphoria is nothing like her name. The town refers to her as kvetching and most folk say she never smiles. Travis's dad says she acts like her shit doesn't stink. If only he knew the truth.

Bethany Lorell

Jessica Schneider

Ever since Mrs. Euphoria Rivers left town, my world has crumbled to pieces. Actually, it was not the Dodge Dart that Mrs. Rivers left in that drove through my heart; the Shitlist was the dynamite. So, a woman-shaped crater lies in my chest and becomes more infected by the day. People did not expect the Shitlist, least of all on their own doorsteps. Some of the scrawled names belong to people who had practically begged for Mrs. Rivers' retaliation. That is why I cannot understand why *Bethany Lorell*, my beloved name for all twenty-three years of my life, was written in malevolent cursive alongside those of wicked people who tortured her tirelessly. What did I ever do?

I always wanted to be a veterinarian. Animals are loyal, kind, and everything a person would want in a friend. Human friends, I have realized, are never trustworthy or easily understood. The Shitlist taught me that. And pets have the decency to only judge people internally and not say it to their faces. Well, except for parrots. Becoming a veterinarian is not an easy feat, however. To gain some experience, I became a dog groomer.

It turns out, spreading the word of my startup business "Lorell Pet Grooming!" provided its own challenges. Quonsettville is a town of animal lovers, but most of those people are like guard dogs for their pet guard dogs. What I mean is, I had to work hard to earn their trust.

"This is WVOC 91.3FM, your *classic* station for *classic*al music! Folks, for our February 'Community Notices Program,' I'm joined now by 23-year-old Bethany Lorell, the business-woman behind 'Lorell Pet Grooming!'" It feels so long ago since I started working on my passion project. It was definitely this radio interview that greased the squeaky wheels.

"Thank you," I had said. "This means a lot to me, especially after a long day of stuffing flyers in mailboxes!"

"How about you tell us about your company."

"Well, I love, love, *love* pets, and I feel like it's a great way to give back to the animal kingdom!" I said, chattering. "And I want to be a vet someday, so when I become one, you will know I'm really qualified! My studio is located in a trailer by Coolidge Avenue. Though it is small, it is filled to its limit with love and care!"

"Thank you, Bethany. Well, there you have it folks. 'Lorell Pet Grooming' is the next big pet barbershop in Quonsettville, so get ahead of the trend! This is WVOC 91.3FM, and continue having a *classic* day," the radioman concluded.

Just two hours after I left the stuffy recording studio for my air-conditioned apartment, phone calls rushed in. It reached the point where I even started to feel annoyed at my trendy K-Pop ringtone. But business is business, and business was booming. By March, my six hours a day, five days a week work schedule was as solid as diamond. I even had a generous customer on Sundays who paid me twice the amount most people did for the same job.

The funny thing is, I met my favorite client not at my makeshift office, but along my Sunday jog. I saw Mrs. Rivers at the library while checking out every book I could find relating to veterinarian work, but I did not know of her dog. The day I saw Mrs. Rivers, I was shivering as I jogged around the frozen layer of ice that sat on top of Quonsett Pond protecting it from the world. I ran into her while she was walking her beloved Clover. Jogging the outskirts of the serene pond, basking in the idyllic environment, has always made me feel at peace. It is hard to say now whether I will run that path again.

"Good day, Mrs. Rivers! And who do we have here?" The thrill in my voice was obvious as it sang its way across the space between us.

"This is Clover, an 18-month-old rescue golden retriever. And you must be Bethany Lorell, the young woman on the radio!" Mrs. Euphoria Rivers replied. My pleasant surprise at the recognition must have been apparent because she continued, "It's that lovely, distinct voice of yours."

My business side rose up and I said, "Would you like to be a part of the 'Lorell Pet Grooming!' family? I am customer-friendly, helpful ..." The words sagged like rough cardboard on my tongue, the blandness of the speech tasting like sandpaper. Mrs. Rivers seemed oblivious to the quiet pattering of my words dying off; if she was, her expression remained warm and polite.

"Sure, Miss Lorell. Here is my phone number ..." We exchanged contact information, and friendship blossomed.

Clover was my favorite pet customer, but it was always disappointing when Mrs. Rivers' husband P.P. brought her into the trailer rather than Mrs. Rivers herself. To compensate, I made sure I saw Mrs. Rivers as much as possible. It was tough to give up my great Sunday client, but I decided to clear my schedule in order to jog when Mrs. Rivers was walking Clover. Both seemed to love the company. I always felt better after those runs knowing that Mrs. Rivers and I were forging a connection.

As time passed, spidery cracks formed in the ice as it crumbled and thawed, revealing the blue sheen beneath. May's arrival awakened the pond's ferry, and crowds flocked to the dock. The ferry did not touch Clover's walks, nor did it affect my jogging schedule. Therefore, we ignored the ferry and ran our mile along the pond as usual. I thought that would never change.

One day was different. I was pushing my aching body through a strenuous jog around the pond when a familiar-looking dog bounded towards me, and I bent down for Clover to jump into my arms and lick my face.

"Clover!" I said with a massive grin across my face.

As the dog came closer and her face became clear, I realized my mistake. There was something unfamiliar about this dog's face. Maybe the puppy's slightly discolored eyes were what made me realize this dog was not Clover. To make matters worse, I turned around to see a dog with Clover's *actual* eye color staring at me. Though the real Clover looked despondent, her expression was nothing compared to Mrs. Rivers'.

Her eyes were flaming with the fury of a thousand captive demons from Hell.

(So whenever I see a relatively small golden retriever, I look at it three times, like a small child crossing the street, to make sure it is the dog I am looking for.)

Going to Municipal Library soon became my work break. I learned that F. Scott Fitzgerald is one of Mrs. Rivers' favorite authors after (accidentally) listening to a conversation between her and someone checking out his works, so I would always greet her with one of his quotes.

"'Her voice is full of money.' Good morning, Mrs. Rivers!" I said one day in the library. I was desperate for more quotes. That day was particularly busy, so I had hoped to cheer her up.

"Morning."

"Hey, I was wondering if I could take you out to dinner tonight! It could be fun, just you and me – and Clover if she's up for it." Ever since the day we ran into each other by Quonsett Pond, I had tried to arrange a dinner outing.

"I'm busy, Bethany," Mrs. Rivers said promptly. It felt odd that her sentences seemed to coil up like a Slinky as time passed. In the back of my mind, I wondered what would happen if it sprung. If the Shitlist is any indication, I would not want to be in the coil's way.

An idea-lightbulb almost blinded me, so I said eagerly, "Oh! I can help behind the desk! I can check out books or hand you library cards or print out receipts or –"

"Stop! Bethany, just go."

Maybe that should have been my warning sign to stay away for good.

But I took it as a cry for help.

So I began to brainstorm brilliant ideas for how to massage the tension out of Mrs. Rivers. Then, I had the perfectly round sketched circle of a thought: I would make her a gift box! It was the perfect plan, the cherry on top of our fabulous, minty and chocolatey friendship. And I had an idea on just what to put in it. She gardened, so I decided it would be botanically themed.

"Mrs. Rivers! Mrs. Rivers!" My knuckles rapped emphatically against her front door on W. Robespierre Street, "I have something for you!"

"Bethany? What are you *doing* here?"

"Giving you a present!"

"Oh, how very thoughtful. But you best be going now, as you must have lots to do." Her words seemed kind, but her candy smile seemed to be more rotten than sweet.

"Not at all! I could stay all day!" I said happily.

"Well, thank you for the lovely gift." Mrs. Rivers quickly shut the door. I knocked again.

"*What?*" she asked, and I sensed the tightness of a pulled rubber band in her voice.

"Don't you want to open the gift while I'm here?"

"Not particularly." When she closed the door this time, the forceful slam rattled the house, as if the home itself was shaking its head.

Mrs. Rivers stopped answering my calls.

She stopped responding to my texts.

The last Sunday before Mrs. Rivers left Quonsettville, I turned around the bend to watch the ferry go by. I was not going to ride it, but the ripples and splashes of water around it and smiles on passengers' faces made it fun to watch. By then, I was perplexed as to why Mrs. Rivers had not met up with me yet. Just as I decided she must be sick, I saw a golden retriever on the ferry. I looked three times, and it was definitely Clover, and Mrs. Rivers was by her side. There must have been a reasonable explanation for why she was riding the ferry to Bridalvale, so I smiled and waved. She looked away.

I hate conflict, but Mrs. Rivers was disinterested in making an effort in applying reconciliation glue to our relationship's splintering wooden supports. Somehow, I even believed this was my fault. I have to remind myself it was I who extended the olive branch and made an effort. Mrs. Rivers did not care; it was all for naught.

Then, Mrs. Rivers skipped town. She wanted to leave, so be it. That does not justify blaming people, least of all me, for her departure, especially in such a bluntly rude fashion. This was another door slammed in my face, but this time all of Quonsettville saw it happen. It makes sense to hate Mrs. Rivers. Sometimes I do. The worst part is that every F. Scott Fitzgerald quote, every golden retriever, and every pink car reminds me of her. Whenever my voice grows taut and my words cling tightly together, ready to spring apart, I remember Mrs. Rivers. Her memory blares in my head and I need to let go. There will be another Clover, another Dodge, another librarian. This will be over eventually, I know it.

A Flick of the Wand

Patience Mackarness

While other girls my age fixated on Justin Bieber, I dreamed of broomsticks streaking across the night sky. After I showed up at three fancy-dress parties dressed as a witch, someone asked if our family was too poor to buy proper costumes. I won a school art contest; my black paper figure flying in front of a tinfoil moon was called *creepy* by the kid in second place, which pleased me.

My witch phase started right after Nana died. Nana was round and little and not a bit witchy to look at, but she did make potions in her pressure cooker, cough syrups and indigestion remedies that she sold in local markets. I helped her. She told me once that if she'd lived a few centuries ago, she'd have been in big trouble because back then, witches were burned at the stake. I imagined a row of steaks and witches, barbecuing side-by-side over charcoal.

The smell of Nana's potions was still in the kitchen when we cleared out her house; like lavender, with something magically tart underneath. It felt like she was around somewhere, maybe out in the garden snipping herbs. I wondered if there was a spell that would bring her back, and whether I could find it by looking through her books, the ones with leather covers that smelt like old bookstores; but Dad said they all had to be sold like the house, because we needed every cent. He and Mom were fighting a lot just then, mostly about money. I wished Nana was there to tell them to *grow up and think of the child.*

I'd seen *Harry Potter* and *The Wizard of Oz*, so I knew there were good witches as well as bad ones, but I had no time for simpering Glinda and her sparkly wand. Miss Price in *Bedknobs and Broomsticks* was something else. I loved the apprentice witch in tweeds, who starts out prim and crabby but has a heart of gold for the kids staying in her home. I watched the DVD over and over. It was Mom who said, if I loved that story so much, why not read the book? That's how I came to be in Quonsettville Library one Friday after school.

Most people preferred to ask Florry Fayette if they needed help, but I walked right up to Mrs Rivers where she sat behind her desk, looking beaky and fierce. I said loudly, "I want *Bedknobs and Broomsticks*, please."

Mrs Rivers looked at me over the top of her glasses, gold-rimmed and hung on a fine gold chain. Her cardigan was mauve lambswool, but her skirt could have been tweed.

I added, so there could be no doubt, "There's a witch in it."

Mrs Rivers said in her sharp, precise voice, "There is indeed, Eve. And for your information, there are *two* books. One is called *The Magic Bedknob*, the other is called *Bonfires and Broomsticks*."

Pure Miss Price. Wonderful.

Back home, I found surprises in the books, like Emilius being a necromancer from the seventeenth century, nothing like the shabby con man in the movie. The part where he was nearly burned as a witch gave me the chills, but when Miss Price saved his life, I loved her more than ever. And I liked that she made mistakes, forgetting spells and falling off her broomstick. Like Nana, when she forgot someone's name and said *Oh, silly me!* and smacked her own bottom with the newspaper.

I started visiting the library most Fridays, and asking Mrs Rivers to recommend books. I think it pleased her to do it. The books she suggested were old-fashioned, maybe ones she'd read when she was young herself. They were mostly about rebellious girls who calmed down after they married strong men, or did something heroic and were made Head Girl at school. Mrs Rivers used to talk to me about the books when I brought them back, and at first it felt like she was testing me, but sometimes her face would change as if she was remembering things that made her happy. She didn't talk about spells or magic, but then, neither did Miss Price; the children had to work out her secret for themselves. One day, when the library was about to close, Mrs Rivers said suddenly, "Never let anyone tell you the kind of person you should be, Eve. Be sure to follow your own star." As she spoke, the lights flashed off and on six times. Mrs Rivers humphed and said the fusebox was playing up again. But I knew.

The next Friday, a boy my age came into the children's section while his parents were filling up at the gas station. He took down a book and started scribbling in it. Mrs Rivers told him to stop, but he stuck out his tongue at her. She said slowly and softly, so only the boy and I could hear, "People who deface books in libraries will come to a sticky end, young man." He looked scared for a moment; then he deliberately drew a heavy black line across the title page of *Tom's Midnight Garden*. He stood up with a loud scrape of chair-legs on the polished floor, and walked out. A few minutes later, we all heard screaming brakes from LaChute Street, followed by a *crunch*, and breaking glass, and a horn that blared on and on. Mrs Rivers strolled over to the window with the rest of us, wearing a little smile.

It was a few weeks later that Delmar Dickerson walked into the pharmacy with a red angry face, and said, "I swear, that

Euphoria Rivers is a witch!" And I said right away, proud of my knowledge, "She certainly is!"

I was waiting in line with Mom, and the pharmacy was full. A couple of people laughed. Mom look shocked, and jabbed me with her elbow. And someone must have told Mrs Rivers, because she called Mom that same evening to complain, and Mom made me go to the library and apologize.

It was horrible. Mrs Rivers didn't look at me when I walked up to her desk. I started stumbling over my words, saying things like *I didn't mean it like that, Mrs Rivers, honestly I never would,* and maybe I'd have gone on to explain about Miss Price and Nana, even though I knew it would make me sound stupid. But Mrs Rivers said to Florry, who looked like she wished she was somewhere else, "Floretta, please tell Eve Durrant that henceforth she is not welcome in this library."

The weird thing was that afterwards, the whole town decided I was some kind of bad-girl celebrity. It turned out I was the first person ever to be banned from the library, though I wasn't the last. All the kids thought that was super cool. All the kids thought it was cool to be banned from the library. Nobody had ever thought I was cool before. Now if anyone asked, I laughed and said Mrs Rivers had made me read lame books about goody-goody girls who got married and lived happily ever after. And I told them the creepy way she'd smiled when the boy had his accident.

Other things were changing too. Dad finally left, which meant no more fights between him and Mom, but plenty between Mom and me. I started hanging around with kids who smoked and played hooky. I grew boobs, and swore a lot. I experimented with boys, and with magic mushrooms we picked in the woods. I went to a party as a punk rocker, in a tight black leather skirt with a bike chain for a belt, and a string of safety-pins in my earlobe. When Mom said she didn't like the person I was turning into, I snapped back *You're just jealous because I have a life!*

I kept reading, though. I went to the library in Burlington, which was bigger than the one in Quonsettville. At first I chose books I'd heard were dirty or shocking, like *Tropic of Cancer* and *A Clockwork Orange*. Later I decided it was OK to read things because I liked them, and wanted to know about the stuff that was in them. I found that worked with people too.

This fall, I'm going away to college. I'm excited and a little bit scared. Mom and I think it will do us good to be apart for a while. She and Dad both say they're proud of me.

I haven't seen Mrs Rivers since she left town, but one night I dreamed about her. She was being cooked on a barbecue, and I was the chef, and a long line of people were waiting for their share. But she didn't seem to mind being barbecued, and when I prodded her with a fork, she wriggled and squealed with laughter.

Jean-Pierre Pelletier

Rachael Dickzen

It was really only by happenstance that I found out about the Shitlist at all. I work at home and avoid most attempts at socialization. Everyone in Quonsettville knows everyone else's business anyway; I don't have any desire to make their job easier. But on that particular day in June, when the Shitlist started flying across town, I had been forced to leave the safety of my house by a broken Mr. Coffee.

When I walked into Evita's, the bell clanging as it hit the glass door, the morning crowd was already buzzing with excitement. Several people leaned over their phones at the counter, studying them like college students before an exam.

I ordered my coffee quietly, but unfortunately, someone noticed me.

"Riley!" called someone I Definitely should have recognized but Definitely did not. "Have you heard the news?" I shook my head, hoping that would end the exchange, but she beckoned me over. I joined her and tried to look polite.

This woman told me the whole story in hushed tones, with the occasional contribution from other nosy nellies around us. These aspiring detectives pored over the grainy pictures of the notorious document, wondering at each name and comparing notes.

I asked if anyone knew how her family was handling her disappearance, but no one answered.

"Do you know anything, Riley?" they asked. "Can you look at the list?"

I had no intention of telling these clucking hens anything, but I looked anyway. Jean-Pierre Pelletier's name was right there, as I expected. I was there, after all, when he earned his spot.

As soon as I got my coffee, I murmured my thanks and skedaddled. As I headed back down LaChute, I thought back to how it all started.

As usual, I had been holed up in my mom's old house out near the Quackquois, writing semi-diligently. My computer is positioned in front of a large window, so I can gaze out at the historic tannery's white brick walls when I'm looking for inspiration (aka, procrastinating). I could hear Mrs. Rivers' car coming up Old Tannery Lane long before it came into sight; that dratted Dart has the loudest rattle in town.

When I next looked up, she was at the tannery door, talking with my new neighbor, who held a doily-covered plate of cookies in his giant hands. Sporting a skull-covered shirt, he squinted down at the wrinkled and dimpled Euphoria. Her gray hair was coiffed into a particularly high helmet that day, as if for battle.

I watched, tapping my pen. I knew Euphoria from the library; I ventured there every few weeks for a new helping of mystery novels. She had always been unrelentingly kind. Yet only a few sentences into their conversation, it looked like things were heating up. Euphoria's smile had vanished and now she looked positively aghast. I pushed the window up just enough to hear.

"You want to paint flames on a 225-year-old building?" Euphoria asked. If she had pearls, she would've been clutching them.

"Why not?" Jean-Pierre responded. He grabbed a cookie and took a defiant bite.

"My ancestor Théophille LaChute was Quonsettville's George Washington; this tannery is our Mount Vernon." Her voice sounded strangled as she struggled to remain calm.

"Washington would say I can do what I want on my own property," he shot back, stuffing the rest of the cookie into his mouth. He nodded to himself, satisfied with his retort.

Euphoria sighed and tried another tactic. "The tannery is on the state historic register. You can't make any major changes without their approval, or you could face serious fines."

"How are they going to know? They're off in Stowe or wherever."

"Montpelier," Euphoria supplied flatly. "Vermont's capital. But they'll know, as I'm calling them about this as soon as I get back to the library!" Her voice rose a couple notches.

I wondered if I had time to make popcorn.

"I wouldn't do that if I were you," Jean-Pierre replied, tense, his mouth twisting into a frown.

"I must protect Mount Vernon!!" she shrieked.

The big man's face twisted in fury. "Get off my property!" he shouted, wrenching at the doorknob.

"I will!" Euphoria yelled at the slamming door. "Happily!"

She stalked away, and then paused at her car before shifting toward my house. I jumped away from the window.

The knock at my door came a moment later. Conscious of my grubby sweatpants, I opened it and pasted on a smile.

"Hello Riley, dear. I need a favor." She paused, waiting for a response. I stared back until she continued. "As you know,

I'm vice-president of the Historical Preservation League. We're concerned that your neighbor may do something drastic to the tannery."

"Like what?" I feigned innocence.

"Well, one of my patrons was in the other day, and he mentioned that Jean-Pierre was asking about who in town could paint a mural. I just came to talk, to make sure he was abiding by the requirements for historic buildings, and wouldn't you know it, he wants to paint flames all over it in honor of some Panther band!"

"Pantera?" I asked.

"Maybe." She waved the name away impatiently. "I explained that the tannery is on the historic registry, but he just wouldn't listen. I'm afraid he might do it anyway. Could you be a dear and call if you see a painter?" She shoved a pink business card my way.

I took it with a doubtful hand. "I don't know, Mrs. Rivers; I don't want any trouble."

"It won't be any trouble; I'll leave your name out of it and he'll never know it's you. Just call me if you see anything."

"But no one else lives out here ..." I began, but Euphoria was already thanking me and waving a farewell.

Soon, Jean-Pierre was trying to recruit me to his side of the flame war. One evening, while bingeing Netflix and typically drinking wine with my cat, I heard a heavy pound on my door.

Jean-Pierre stood there, sporting yet another skull-covered shirt. He clearly had An Aesthetic. "Hi. We haven't met yet, but I'm Jean-Pierre Pelletier. I inherited the tannery next door from my great-uncle. Can we talk?" I sighed and nodded, sipping my wine.

"I just want to run my business – I'm teaching leather tanning classes to survivalists, for when society falls apart – and do what I want with my own property, but some nosy old lady has been harassing me," he said.

I gave a non-committal "mmhm." I needed significantly more alcohol to deal with this.

"I'm going to the Board of Selectmen on Thursday to ask them to take my home off the historic registry."

I thought this was foolish, since the registry was run by Vermont, not Quonsettville, but I kept quiet. If my neighbor wasn't capable of googling that information, I didn't feel the need to help him discover it.

"Could you come be my witness? Say I'm a good neighbor?"

"Um, I'd rather not get involved …" I stammered.

"Please consider it? I could use your help." At that, he left. Pondering, I sipped wine in his wake. He hadn't even asked my name.

I did not attend the Board meeting, of course. Wild horses could not have dragged me, not even wild horses with free wine and cheese. I stayed in and read a book instead.

I have no idea what happened at that meeting. Let's be honest, the selectmen probably just stared at Jean-Pierre blankly. But a few days before Euphoria's disappearance, I woke up to the sound of shouts. Half-asleep, I ran outside. I immediately regretted this decision.

Town handyman Delmar Dickerson stood there, mouth gaping as he stared at Euphoria, who brandished a paint roller.

She was yelling at Jean-Pierre, who approached with a menacing paint can.

"I'm not giving this back, you nitwit! You'll only use it to defile the tannery!"

"I can defile it if I want!" he roared. "And your cookies are dry as plaster dust!"

She gasped. "Philistine!"

Just then, he saw me, barefoot and sporting my fanciest t-shirt and boxers.

"Call the police!" Jean-Pierre bellowed. "She's stealing my property!"

"Yes, DO call the police, Riley!" Euphoria shouted. "This man is about to ruin a priceless piece of history! And my outfit!"

I gawked as they continued to shout at each other, calling each other all sorts of ridiculous names. Then I walked back inside, locking the door tightly. I turned away from the window, grabbed my headphones, and put on a loud podcast to drown out the noise.

Eventually the clatter of Euphoria's Dart stirred me from my murder podcast reverie. I peeked through the window. Only Delmar remained, hosing paint off the grass. Red was splattered across the tannery's white bricks like a Jackson Pollack murder scene. The paint roller was conspicuously absent.

The librarian's car rattled off into the distance until I could hear it no more.

The Shitty Exchange

Samuel Gulliksson

When Theresa told me what Three-Pee did, I couldn't stop myself from laughing. My daughter, who's always been a prude – something she definitely inherited from her mother – looked at me with an angry face.

"Oh, come on honey. It was kinda funny."

"It was totally inappropriate!"

"Yes, dear. You're right."

"Someone should really do something about it. It isn't the first time he's acted so indecent."

Trying to appease her – to avoid it turning into a long-drawn argument keeping me from funny YouTube videos of dogs not wanting to take a bath – I promised I would be the one trying to do something about it:

"I could have a talk with his grandma. She comes in the shop every Saturday afternoon."

When the next Saturday rolled around, Euphoria Rivers entered the butcher shop I took over from my father twenty years ago. 3.25pm on the dot, as usual. Always five minutes before closing, regardless if she was on her way home from the library or if she had the day off; you could set a clock by her. She asked for four lamb chops for Sunday dinner, as usual. I wrapped them up in white butchers' paper – just as my dad used to do – and while she grabbed her pocketbook to pay, I tried to come up with some way to mention Theresa's encounter with Three-Pee.

"Theresa told me she got... Eerm, let's just say she saw more of Three-Pee than she bargained for in broad daylight."

"What do you mean?"

"On her way out from Kale Express the other day she saw Three-Pee in his car. Or mostly his bare ass pressed against the passenger window."

Woops! That didn't come out nearly as delicately as I intended, and I still couldn't keep myself from cracking up at the thought of Three-Pee mooning down entire Lorraine Street. Euphoria didn't seem to share my amusement. Instead she gasped and I watched her thin eyebrows fly a whole half-inch closer to her hairline.

"Three-Pee would never do that!"

"Apparently, he did. And my daughter didn't find it very funny."

"Of course your neurotic daughter didn't! She's always thought herself too good for this town."

"Don't talk like that about my daughter! It's not like this is the first time Three-Pee –"

"You are accusing my grandson –"

"I'm not accusing him. I'm just telling you what my daughter told me."

"You are spreading falsehoods! Just as you are with these!"

Euphoria shook the package of lamb chops at me and continued:

"If it weren't for my loyalty to local business, I'd have stopped buying your overpriced meat a long time ago... No wonder your daughter prefers Kale Express!"

"What's that supposed to mean?"

"It doesn't look very good when the butcher's daughter is vegan."

As if attacking my life's work wasn't enough, ridiculing me and my daughter – that was it!

"You're one to speak! What you call 'dance class' is a sham! An inflatable tube man could just as well teach it."

I couldn't help but smirk as I watched Euphoria's face turn red. But then she quickly straightened her already perfect scarf around her neck and snorted.

"Without me, this town would be nothing!"

"Hah! We managed just fine before you returned and started sticking your nose in everything."

"I don't have to listen to this!"

Euphoria slammed exact change for the lamb chops on the counter and stormed out from the shop, leaving a faint flowery scent after her. My father's words – and the bane of every service worker's existence – started ringing in my head: "the customer is always right". Just a bit too late now, I guess.

The next afternoon I dragged Butterball for a walk across the Quackquois River to swanky Quonsett Cascade in the rain. She didn't like to be out in the rain and would have rather stayed home, so I coaxed her with a never-ending stream of treats on the brisk march towards W. Robespierre Street. The genius idea had come to me during our early morning walk; there could be another use for the command I'd taught her to minimise the time we spent out in the cold in the winter.

I stopped right in front of Euphoria's house and issued the magic words: "go potty." Not very original, I know, but it did the trick. All the treats on the way over must have taken effect; Butterball managed to leave a not insignificant steaming pile just on the edge of the lawn despite being a small Bichon Frisé.

As I glanced towards the house, I met Euphoria's horrified eyes. She was standing completely frozen on the front porch with her golden retriever Clover anxiously waiting to go for a walk. Just my luck! I quickly turned around and hurried back the same way we'd arrived, with Butterball trying to keep up behind me.

I went to sleep happy that night, only slightly regretting the childish move. That happiness quickly dissipated the next morning though, when, on my way to work, I was greeted by a huge pile of dogshit at the end of our driveway. Next to it sat a small plastic bag with what I guessed was Butterball's poop from yesterday. Despite Butterball doing her very best, it was no match to what I could only assume was Clover's work.

At least I'd made the oh-so-respectable Mrs. Rivers stoop so low as to be picking up my dog's poop. Or was it the work of her henpecked husband P.P.?

Loretta Lane LaBiché

Benjamin Whitaker

Loretta Lane LaBiché, aptly nicknamed "La Bitch" by her fellow Quonsettville residents, was not a patient woman. She was ambitious, proud, and cutthroat. She didn't care if she was loved, or even liked for that matter, as long as she was better. Superior. And as long as everyone else knew it. And so far, she felt most Quonsettvillians believed she was. Well, except one person in particular.

Mrs. Euphoria Rivers.

Euphoria Rivers had grown up in this town and almost everyone knew her. Loretta, on the other hand, had only moved to Quonsettville from Montpelier only two years ago and didn't quite fit in.

But, as she was very fond of saying, "No matter!" Loretta remained in Quonsettville out of principle and was determined to do what she was here for.

Loretta had a messiah complex. Even though most people may not particularly like her, she desperately wanted to save them. And she believed the best way to do that was to save people from the two greatest threats to humanity: gluten and GMO food products!

Only two weeks after moving to town, she opened Loretta Lane's, a bake shop serving only organic goods. Not a single thing in her shop was genetically modified.

Business boomed: soon she opened a cookbook library in a

sideroom of her bake shop.

Graduating from the University of Vermont in 2014, Loretta spent five years in Montpelier writing cookbooks filled with her own recipes. No publisher would publish them, but now with the money she was making from her own business, she had no problem publishing them herself. She also included many of her personal favorites, including Jessica Alba's *The Honest Life* and Chrissy Teigen's *Cravings*, in her library. For now she would spread healthy lifestyles around Quonsettville.

Then to the world.

Everything was splendid until Euphoria Rivers paid Loretta an official visit.

Loretta was wearing her signature blue and white striped cardigan over a plain white blouse and black shirt. Her silver crucifix necklace hung over her heart. The bistro was packed this morning, all the mahogany wood tables and chairs Loretta had carefully placed on her first day of business filled with people enjoying a late breakfast. She was serving two of her famous blueberry muffins to the last customer of the mid-morning rush when the Chief Librarian entered and headed to the front counter. Loretta would be glad to serve her, but something about the way Euphoria carried herself made Loretta nervous. She fiddled with her crucifix necklace; she feared she might need God's help to deal with whatever Euphoria was bringing.

"Ms. LaBiché," Euphoria trilled. "May I have a word with you privately?"

Loretta narrowed her eyes before answering. "I'm a little busy, but I suppose." She wiped her hands on a rag, dumped it by the register, and stepped out from behind the counter. She followed Euphoria to her organic library, the only empty spot in the busy bakery.

Euphoria began, "I have a proposition for you."

144

Loretta, forcing a benevolent smile, held up a hand to quiet her. "First of all, Mrs. Rivers, is it? Never have you ever purchased an item in my shop. If I was looking for a business partner, I wouldn't ask you." She folded her hands across her chest.

Euphoria laughed. "I don't desire any part of your millenial baking, Ms. LaBiché."

Loretta's face flushed with anger. Anger was not part of a healthy lifestyle. She tried to think happy thoughts: a beautiful day at the beach, an unlikely friendship between a cat and a dog, gluten-free muffins.

Euphoria waited for Loretta's face to turn back from its current firetruck red. "Let me start over," she said. "I know how civic-minded you are. I know how much you love this community and the people here. I know how much you care about encouraging healthy lifestyles."

"All true," Loretta said.

"I believe," Euphoria continued, "that the best way to accomplish all of your passions is to donate your collection of cookbooks here to the municipal library where I work."

Loretta's jaw dropped. Out of every possible scenario she could have imagined, Euphoria asking to take her books for free was not one of them.

"Let me get this straight: instead of selling these books to help keep my business running, you would rather me just give them away to collect dust in a city library?"

"They won't be gathering dust," Euphoria explained. "Library members will come and check them out and use them, just as you intend. Adding your books to the collection of 47 cookbooks we already have will provide the citizens even more options when starting healthy lifestyles."

Her eyes darted to Loretta's self-published cookbook standing pride-of-place on the shelf beside them.

"And some of your books are a little expensive."

Loretta rolled her eyes. "No one goes to the public library!" she snapped. Heads twisted in their direction.

"We actually have a rather large number of members who check books out regularly," Euphoria explained. "Your books will not go unread."

"Frankly, I don't believe you," Loretta responded. Those who had turned at Loretta's outburst moments ago turned away, losing interest in the argument.

"Just consider it," Euphoria said. "Think it over for a day or two and we can talk more." Euphoria dug into her pocketbook and finding a pink business card, held it out to Loretta.

"No," Loretta said, not taking the card. "Now if you're quite done wasting my time, I need to get back to work." Loretta turned sharply on her heel and marched away behind the counter to the kitchen, not giving Euphoria a second glance

Loretta let out a breath. She sipped her lemon balm tea, then stepped into the pantry and pulled down the ingredients for caraway seed and lemon muffins.

So some old lady thinks she can cheat me out of all my hard work? Loretta thought.

She ripped open the package of muffin mix.

I wasn't born yesterday.

She chopped the lemons on her granite cutting board.

I know better.

She dumped the ingredients together and started mixing.

Yet another thing she felt superior about.

New Rule at the Post Office

Shanique Burton

Salome slammed her fists onto the cluttered desk: where the hells bells is Albert? She had been punching keys and clicking icons ham-fisted for the past forty-five minutes without a successful outcome.

Although she had written countless letters in opposition to the upgrade, making the point that the post office could in fact remain efficient without the help of technology, her complaints were rendered void by the green campaign.

Nevertheless, Salome abdicated and made a commitment to accommodate the change as best as she could but it seemed the wretched computer didn't want a truce. From the moment it was delivered the brute had declared war on her. It refused to respond to her touch. It wouldn't "startup" or "load a webpage" or "open a file" so long as she was sitting in front of it. A simple thing as sending an email would take her an hour. Meanwhile, the tech-savvy intern Albert Tinmore would click-click-click and just like that – email sent!

Ttnnnnuup, ttnnnnuuup, ttnnnnnnuuuuuuup.

There it went again. After her sixth attempt at trying to answer the phone Salome decided she would leave it to Albert. She suspected the phone colluded with the computer to make her job harder but whenever she tried to make that argument, it would be refuted.

"Your only problem Ms. Sullivan, is that you just don't like technology." Albert's familiar response would stimulate Salome's narrow-eyed death stare.

"Whether I like it or not is beside the point, I shouldn't have to use all the laws of quantum physics to answer one simple phone call." With that, Salome would leave the conversation regardless of whether the conversation continued.

So the phone rang. It rang like a child throwing a tantrum and she ignored it like a mother administering discipline.

She was about to use her cell phone to call Albert when he sauntered through the staff entrance. He was five feet ten inches of portly appearance and few words, never to be seen without his lunch tote. Ever so gracefully, he rested his bag on the small table provided for him. It was an old wooden table that might have been a donation from the Quonsettville Middle School, considering the abundant wads of stale gum beneath it.

The post office was small: a miniature reception area at the front and behind that, a mail sorting room and the general administrative room where Salome had her "office" – she didn't like to call it that because she had no doors to close. Staffed only with two permanent workers – Salome Sullivan and Zavier Willoughby the mailman – the post office was not designed for a larger workforce, but since Albert's internship was only six months long, more sophisticated furniture was unnecessary.

At the request of Salome, he performed the magical flickering of his fingers as if he had a private agreement with the keyboard and before Salome could ask *How'd you do that?* he was through. No questions asked, no explanations given. He had an urgent appointment with a homemade bacon-sausage breakfast Panini.

She didn't like that about him. It was fortunate that Albert started his internship on the same day as the delivery of the computer because she wouldn't have survived with it on her own. Zavier was himself computer-literate, but he was always out delivering mail whenever she needed help to conquer the computer. She needed to actually learn to master the monster before it was too late, but how could she learn anything if he made a habit of giving her the fish rather than handing her the rod once in a while?

It would be a good time to ask for lessons, she thought: two hours per day, three times weekly. By the time she was halfway through her rationale, the purring of Zavier's scooter interrupted her thoughts, and before she could begin her address to Albert he was inside the office with Mrs. Euphoria Rivers practically at his heels, clutching a black leather bag under her arm.

"Good morning, Mrs. Rivers," Salome said, peeved at her presence. The one thing Salome detested more than working without a proper office was the unannounced visits from locals. Despite her numerous attempts at establishing a boundary, some people never thought it necessary to use the reception area.

Salome turned her attention to Zavier who now stood before her, guzzling down some water from a bottle. "Zavier, you know we have rules, why didn't you show Mrs. Rivers the proper way to enter the post office?"

"She wanted to talk to you," he answered. Then gulped more water.

Salome had taken a stance never to serve anybody unless they entered through the correct door, and she didn't plan on going against her word. As a matter of fact, she went as far as a sign that read:

THIS IS A PRIVATE OFFICE,
ALL CUSTOMERS WILL BE SERVED
ONLY AT THE RECEPTION DESK.

The laminated copy was placed on the door for trespassers to see and another stuck on the wall behind her desk.

"Mrs. Rivers," Salome began, "I mean no disrespect, but I must insist that you go around to the reception area and I will be with you shortly."

"You're asking me to leave?" Euphoria replied.

"Not in a full sense, just to go around to reception, I will meet you there." Salome did her best to hide her annoyance: her eye squint and tightly-pressed lips gave her away. She and Mrs. Rivers had once been schoolmates, but that didn't exempt her from the rule.

"But I'm already here."

"That's the rule, Mrs. Rivers," Salome cocked her head backwards, "it's right there on the wall." She rose from her chair, stepped past a filing cabinet in front of her desk and said, over her shoulder, "I will be right here waiting to assist you."

"I am here to make a complaint, I demand that you speak to me at once," Euphoria said, switching the bag from one arm to the other.

Salome cleared her throat and fidgeted with her wrist.

"You better go around the front, ma'am, that's the rule," said Zavier. Usually he would take care to stay out of such an encounter, but he was just as annoyed that she had followed him into the office without his consent.

Euphoria let out a breath as strong as a tornado and stomped out of the room, appearing seconds later at the reception desk. "Does *this* satisfy you?"

"Well hello, Mrs. Rivers, how can I help you today?" asked Salome with a wide grin.

"I Al-Rea-Dy told you, I've come to make a complaint –"

"You have to fill out a complaint form," Salome said, leaving Euphoria mid-sentence, mouth open, to fetch the form. She returned with a short piece of paper and slid it across to her.

"I was just about to tell you, Ms. Sullivan," Mrs. Rivers protested, her words short and sharp, "I have already completed two of those forms. I will not complete another one."

"Then I will have to check the file. Once I've read the complaint, I will do my best to resolve the matter. Would you like a response by email to support our new no paper policy?" Salome spoke like a robot.

"No, No, No, NO, NO," Euphoria erupted, "if anybody around here had the decency to pick up the phone, I wouldn't be here now. I am simply asking you to stop delivering personal mail to me at my place of work." Her eyes were bulging and her lips quivered as she finished.

Meanwhile, Salome sucked her lips between her teeth to stop herself from telling Euphoria that the post office was not a place for kids. Instead she clasped her fingers behind her and said, "I don't understand your complaint. It was Albert who implemented the new system for his internship project which will be finished in just two and a half weeks." She loosened her fingers as she continued, "It was duly posted on the notice board, but I thought you would have read it, being a librarian. Besides, it's a smart idea to give people their mail while they're at work, it's just like delivering lunch – convenient and on time."

"Not when you work at a Library. I can't have Zavier disturbing the peace every day, with that noisy motorcycle delivering mail that could be put in the P.O box I pay so much to rent."

"You don't get mail every day, Mrs. Rivers, it shouldn't be an inconvenience."

"I beg to differ," said Euphoria as she removed her bag from under her arm and emptied it on the reception desk. "This is just the mail I have collected since Monday."

It was Thursday morning.

There can't be less than thirty, Salome estimated: four letters, eight magazines, five books, twelve bills and three receipts for registered mail, all sorted and bound neatly with rubber bands.

She couldn't help herself. "Oh, dear lord," she said. "Mrs. Rivers why don't you have those emailed to you? Haven't you heard we're going green?"

ome is where the eart is

Lance Manion

Quonsettville's Chief Librarian, disagreed. It should have been a minor issue but over the years it grew into something bigger.

And dumber.

It started with Orville, both big and dumb, and his former career choice. Like so many residents of this quiet Vermont community, he was retired. He spent his days evenly split between sitting at the Notre-Dame Tea Room telling tall tales about his former life as an Elvis impersonator and sitting quietly reading in the municipal library. Now pushing seventy, he still sported big muttonchops and lived by the credo "Taking care of business."

Or, as he would often say, "Taking care hof business." But more on that later.

If you're getting the idea that he dwelled on his past you would not be wrong, and that rubbed some folks the wrong way. If you're wondering why he said "hof" you're obviously itching for this story to get going, which sort of rubs me the wrong way ... but I'm going to suppress my righteous indignation – you certainly wouldn't be nudging Dan Brown to get to the point already – and get to the point already.

Orville had a problem with the letter H. It began when he was young and has continued his entire life.

The problem? He refused to start a word that began with the letter H with the letter H. He would simply omit the letter.

To balance the cosmic scales he would start any word that began with the letter O with an H.

When introducing himself he would say "Horville. Horville. Anson."

This annoyed a lot of people, including a boatload of Elvis fans over the years and, more relevant to the story, one Chief Librarian.

Luckily there was little talking tolerated at the library, but it occasionally would flare up when the two of them bumped into each other in town. Particularly when Orville was holding court at the café, the very same café that Euphoria frequented for lunch due to its close proximity to the library. Having traveled a lot more than most residents, he would spin endless yarns about his time in Vegas and the debauchery that transpired during his many cross-country tours.

"Hello, Horville," she would begin.

"The name is Horville," he would reply, sounding an awful lot like The King.

Everyone braced themselves for what was sure to follow.

"Are you telling everyone about the glory days of singing *Eartbreak Otel?*" she would start in.

"Are you making fun of my speech impediment?" he would counter.

"It's not a speech impediment, Horville. It's a decision to misuse the English language," she would counter. "A conscious decision."

"Since I was a kid?" he would thunder.

"According to you!" she would rethunder.

"Do you really think I enjoyed singing *Ound Dog* and *Awaiian Sunset?* It cost me gigs! I could ave been uge" he would say in a houtraged tone (crap, now he has me doing it).

"Huge. You could have been huge, Orville."

There would typically be a pause while both parties debated continuing the exchange. Typically, they would decide to continue the exchange. Typically, people were happy they did, as it usually got better after the opening salvos.

There would be personal attacks and nasty inferences made. In a small town this passed for entertainment. But then, one fateful day, a light suddenly shone in Euphoria Rivers' eyes. She looked, unironically, euphoric.

"Orville... did you ever play in Horegon?" she inquired.

He nodded to the affirmative, pushing down his anger at her slight.

"Hoklahoma?"

Nod.

"Hohio?"

"What's your point, Mrs. Rivers?" he asked.

"When you played these places, did you sing *Heartbreak Hotel* and *Hound Dog*?"

"You know I did," he replied, wondering what she was getting at.

"But you sang them as *Eartbreak Otel* and *Ound Dog* correct?"

"That is correct," he finally said.

"But you say things that begin with an O with an H don't you?" she said and a small smile crept across her face. "You say things that begin with an O with an H when you're singing honstage in Horlando? Correct?"

Orville, as big and dumb as advertised, still didn't know what she was driving at. Those around him had put the pieces together and began to shift in their seats uncomfortably.

Finally she came out with it. "Orville ... otel and ound begin with an O. Thus you should pronounce them hotel and hound."

Orville Hanson mulled it over awhile with an I-never-thought-of-it-like-that expression, then attempted to say either word. Unsuccessfully.

"Don't mess with my language," Euphoria finally stated, breaking the tension. Then she swiveled her hips, twitched her upper lip as Presley-esque as she could muster, and said, "Thank you. Thank you very much," before walking out the front door.

"Well ... that was really mean," whispered Gary, owner of the café, to nobody in particular.

The Shitlist, Revisited

Kathryn Hood

June 15, 2019

I'd heard about the damned thing, but never actually seen it. But when I checked my mailbox today, at the bottom of the usual mountain of meaningless crap was a copy of a hand-written page entitled *The Shitlist* containing the names of those with whom Euphoria was allegedly at odds.

And there was my name, underlined in red—Margot Fontenot Patout, purported ballet instructor—along with a note, also in red, saying, "Figured you might be interested in this, Margot!"

Although I'd never intentionally done anything to hurt Euphoria, I knew exactly why she'd included me. And, ironically, it all had to do with ballet.

November 2017 – March 2018

My husband Jean was originally from Vermont and I was from Louisiana. We'd moved to Quonsettville from New Orleans in November of 2017, so Jean could take over the law office of an uncle who'd recently passed away.

I'd studied ballet since I was a kid, was dancing solos at sixteen with the New Orleans Ballet Theatre and by eighteen was their principal ballerina. But eventually, I broke my ankle and could no longer dance professionally. So, I opened a ballet school in Metairie and it had been quite successful.

Euphoria had run a studio in Burlington, Vermont known as Li'l Twirlers Dance Academy which taught, among other things, ballet. Her daughter Cissy took over after Euphoria moved to Quonsettville. Never thinking I'd be in competition with Li'l Twirlers, some forty miles away, I opened Margot Fontenot's School of Ballet in March of 2018.

But ballet students from Li'l Twirlers in Burlington soon began trickling into my studio in Quonsettville. These students' fundamentals were practically non-existent. They didn't know a *plié* from a *jeté*, an *arabesque* from a *pirouette*. Many of them had damaged their feet when they were put in toe shoes without proper preparation. As it turned out, neither Euphoria nor Cissy had any formal ballet training. I didn't say a word, I didn't have to. The parents of the girls had plenty to say. As one outspoken mother put it, "Those two bitches don't know a damned thing about ballet! They've been wasting our daughters' time and stealing our fucking money for years!"

Li'l Twirlers was soon hurting badly. Of course, as far as Euphoria was concerned it had nothing to do with her own incompetence; it was all my fault.

April 2018
Shortly after I opened my studio, the Quonsettville High football coach asked me to give Saturday lessons to his players during spring training to improve their agility. I agreed and thought nothing of wearing my leotard or doing hands-on adjustments to show the boys proper positioning. That's just ballet.

But, as I learned later, Euphoria bribed one of her grand-sons, Garth, to tell the school principal that the way I dressed and touched the players made them uncomfortable. Not surprisingly, the coach decided that perhaps ballet wasn't such a good idea for his players after all.

Losing those lessons wasn't that big a deal. By then I had my hands full with my regular students. Still, once I found out Euphoria was responsible, I wasn't about to let her get away with such mischief.

We lived right across the street from each other. So, late one afternoon, when I saw her come in from work, I walked over. She was all smiles when she met me at the door, but that didn't last long.

"Euphoria," I said, shaking my finger at her. "I know all about you bribing your grandson to tell the school principal I'd been behaving inappropriately with the players I've been giving lessons to. Never mind how I found out, I have it on good authority, and if you ever pull another stunt like this, you'll rue the fucking day, pardon my coonass French, you got crossways with me!"

"Well, I never," Euphoria gasped, then slammed the door in my face.

But what I'd said, as blunt as it was, didn't seem to faze her, or not for long anyway.

October 2018 – April 2019

I had several young boys in my regular classes, but they weren't really strong enough to partner with my advanced female students. For that, I needed larger guys. So, in October of 2018, I advertised free *pas de deux* lessons to high school boys, figuring they'd fall all over themselves to get up close and personal with these girls. And I wasn't disappointed. After a few months' practice, I could see some of these boys were actually good enough to perform in the upcoming April recital.

On the night of the performance, I peeked out at the audience and there sat Euphoria on the front row, dressed to kill. I suspected she was up to no good, but there was nothing I could do at that point. And, sure enough, when the guys came on in the first number, she jumped up, shouted "Oh, my God!" then stomped up the aisle toward the exit, ranting, "Those obscene costumes are so tight you can actually see the boys' privates! It's absolutely disgusting and I will not sit here and watch this pornographic excuse for a ballet!"

A few of her blue-haired buddies trooped out with her, but aside from this brief interruption, the show went well. And during curtain call, when the boys took their bow, they got a standing ovation.

Naturally, I was pleased. As the old saying goes, success is always the best revenge.

June 6 – June 14, 2019

I could go on about her petty attempts to sabotage my studio, but I'll only mention one other, her last.

On Thursday, June 6, 2019, my husband's secretary, Ann Marie, overheard Euphoria gossiping with some of her buddies at a Historical Preservation Association luncheon. What she had to say was a variation of the tale she'd spread about my conduct with the football team. Fortunately, Ann Marie had the presence of mind to activate the recorder on her cell phone and captured most of the conversation which she played for Jean when she got back to the office.

This was on Thursday and Jean, who's not beyond a bit of mischief himself, called Euphoria's husband P.P. the next morning.

"P.P., I've been meaning to talk with you about our wives. They've been at each other's throats over their damned ballet studios and it's gotten totally out of hand. Why don't you come by my office Monday, have lunch with me, and maybe the two of us can put an end to all of this female craziness."

"Well, I really have no idea what you are talking about, old man. But I've never been one to turn down a free lunch either. So, I'll see you Monday."

When P.P. arrived the following Monday, a gourmet spread—compliments of me—had been laid out in Jean's conference room, complete with my good china, crystal, silverware and linen napkins. They served themselves, exchanged a few pleasantries, then Jean cut straight to the chase.

"Euphoria's been spreading some pretty nasty rumors about how my wife conducts her ballet classes, P.P. Margot warned her about it once, but she persists, and what she's been saying is going to have consequences."

Obviously caught off-guard, P.P. looked away momentarily, then, regaining a semblance of his composure, began nibbling at an egg-salad sandwich. "This is the first I've heard of this, Jean," P.P. replied. "I sort of tuned out Euphoria years ago to maintain my sanity."

"Well, why don't we just hear it from the horse's mouth?" Jean interjected, pulling out his secretary's cell phone and playing what Euphoria had said to her friends about me the week before.

P.P. was suddenly at a loss for words, staring vacantly at the half-eaten triangle of egg salad sandwich he held in his left hand.

"Maybe you should hear it again, P.P.," Jean continued. "Because it's going to be Exhibit A in the lawsuit I'm about to file on behalf of my wife against Euphoria for slander. Further, the parents of several girls who took ballet lessons at Li'l

Twirlers have approached me about a suit to recover damages for injuries to their daughters' feet ..."

Jean had more to say, quite a bit more, but before he could continue, P.P. put what was left of his sandwich back on his plate, dabbed at a corner of his mouth with one of my linen napkins, and then, without more, stood and took his leave.

That was on Monday and by Friday, Euphoria's June 11th farewell diatribe to the community was all over town.

June 16, 2019

On reflection, maybe some of the folks on *The Shitlist* did actually mistreat Euphoria. Who knows? But, based on my own experience, I'd say exactly the opposite was probably the case.

At any rate, I smile as I sit here composing a letter to the editor, entitled *The Shitlist, Revisited*, laying out my story. We'll see if Harley has the balls to publish it next Friday.

Catch and Release

Jim Bell

"Yes, sir. Fishing is the key to our growth," Gil Burnett argued before the special committee of the Quonsettville Historical Preservation League. "Théophile LaChute, our courageous town founder, loved to fly fish. Think of the benefits an exhibit showing the joy of fly fishing would create for Quonsettville." Gil played to the historical interests of the four women and two men who made up the special committee. They had put out a call for exhibit proposals for a new dedicated space in the Museé de Théophile LaChute.

"I've been fishin' the waters around Quonsettville for over fifty years, instructing tourists on fly fishing through my On-the-Fly guides services. Catch and release. That's the way we've gotta play it. We lure tourists with the promise of a good fishing experience and hook 'em with our charming Quonsettville hospitality," Gil emphasized with a sharp clap of his hands. "Then, we release 'em so they can come back another day," he said, opening his hands as if he were releasing his catch back into the river of life.

"Thank you, Mr. Burnett," said Stella Burnside, chairwoman for the committee. She turned to Euphoria Rivers. "Mrs. Rivers, the floor is yours. You may present your proposal," she said with a smile. Euphoria rose to address the committee.

"Thank you, madam chairwoman," she acknowledged with a slight bow of her head. She adjusted her glasses with a gentle nudge up the bridge of her nose. "Members of the committee," she began, as her gaze engaged each of the six members. "This display should reflect our community's devotion to history, the arts, music, literature, and culture. It should carry a theme similar to the Quonsettville River Flotilla, which I helped organize for this very Historical Preservation League to commemorate the 225th anniversary of the founding of our town, just last year, in 2018. I argue that the memorial should focus on the community service made by librarians of the past, not on the trade of a dubious fisherman whose interests lie in impaling tourists and snuffing out life with reckless abandon."

Euphoria stared at Gil as if she were sighting a prey through glasses now sitting on the end of her nose. She pressed on with her argument. "Mr. Burnett already has a memorial in the museum. A display of his lures hangs near the photos of Théophile LaChute's fishing exploits. As the committee may recall, the MediCenter on the outskirts of town presented the lures to the museum. They are a collection of Mr. Burnett's handiwork removed from the ears, necks, and arms of fishermen impaled by the hideous creatures. Apparently, his fly patterns are aerodynamically challenging to cast. Do we want to subject our tourists to the wrath of his creations?"

Gil fumed and threw down his lucky fishing hat, a fine example of haberdashery riddled with holes made by his lures. "Those flies tell the long and storied history of fly fishin' in Quonsettville," he pleaded to the committee. "They're modeled after the patterns used by Théophile LaChute. You gotta have finesse and a delicate touch to cast a fly. You're tryin' to fool the fish with your presentation." Gil turned and glared at Euphoria. He was sure she wanted to secure her own legacy with a memorial to Quonsettville's chief librarians. "That's somethin' I'm sure you understand, Euphoria."

Gil made a fist and brought it down on the arm of his chair with a thud. "Besides, those prissy little boats of yours nearly ruined my business! Your river flotsam damaged my reputation!" he shouted. "You're the one who created a mess on the river that day."

Euphoria stabbed an index finger at Gil. "No, it is you, Mr. Burnett, who ruined a memorable event," Euphoria shot back. "Those boats were created with my guidance to celebrate the heritage of our town. I personally designed the intricately embroidered and knitted patterns displayed on the sails. They were created to commemorate significant moments in the history of Quonsettville. You have no appreciation of our heritage."

Everyone in town remembers the encounter of that day. The armada of stylish boats under Euphoria's command had invaded Gil's fly fishing class being held just around a bend in the Quackquois River. Dozens of boats and fishing rods had locked in a mock sea battle. The skirmish ended in a tangle of fishing line, hooks, and shredded lace rigging.

Euphoria held up a torn and tattered sail from the engagement as if presenting exhibit A to a jury. "I'm not at all surprised that the significance of the event would be lost on someone who uses fake enticements to capture his prey," she jabbed, as she pursed her lips.

Gil's blood rose to a boil. "Well, you shoulda' designed sturdier sails!" he shouted out, slapping the arm of his chair. "And I don't keep the fish. I practice catch and release. Everything I hook, I put back in the river to fight another day." Gil wagged his finger at Euphoria. "And don't you doubt for a minute that I wouldn't throw you back if I hooked you."

Euphoria turned away from Gil with a soft "Harrumph" and pulled her cardigan tighter across her breasts.

"Don't forget, folks, I convinced Florenza Fayette to take up fly fishing at the ripe age of eighty," Gil said. "She couldn't see worth a lick. Lookin' at all them tiny words crammed in pages an' all musta' ruined her vision. But she sure could throw a fly line."

"The audacity of the man," Euphoria bellowed out as her body lurched back in mock shock. "Have we forgotten the mysterious circumstances concerning the death of our beloved former chief librarian? Isn't it odd," she pointed out, "that Mr. Burnett's lure and a length of fishing line were found embedded in Florenza Fayette's waders when they discovered her body?"

Gil stood up and kicked at his chair. "Immaterial," the fisherman shouted. "There's plenty of fishermen with my lures hooked in their waders and they're still drinkin' rounds at the Smugglers' Hole Inn."

"Mr. Burnett's flies apparently catch more fishermen than fish," Euphoria said with a smirk. "I understand his prized Black Beauty fly pattern, a hideous collection of splayed hackle hairs and glistening brass, is a creation most fish only admire from a distance."

Back and forth, the two argued throughout the evening. As the hour approached ten o'clock, Mrs. Burnside tapped her empty teacup several times on the table, summoning the meeting to order. "Well, we have heard two very passionate proposals tonight," she said, extending her hands to acknowledge the two combatants. "The esteemed presenters have given the committee much to discuss." Her fellow committee members nodded vigorously in agreement. The chairwoman pointed to the clock on the wall. "However, the hour grows late and I suggest we adjourn for the evening. The committee will consider the proposals presented by Mrs. Rivers and Mr. Burnett and announce its decision next week."

With that, Stella Burnside adjourned the meeting. Gil stormed out, mumbling the often heard litany of swear words he spews when a fish gets away. Euphoria smiled at the committee members, hoping to punctuate the end of her presentation with a little charm.

Unfortunately, any decision on the space will need to wait. Euphoria Rivers has left town. In the days that followed, a quartet of fishermen, wrinkled and weathered with the look of men who had spent decades working outdoors, sat at the bar at the Smugglers Hole Inn.

"Yes, sir, boys. That's the way to fish. Catch and release," Gil shared with the group. "You respect the struggle they give you. That's why you release 'em, so they can fight another day." The men studied the fading foam atop their beers. Then one salty companion asked, "Say, Gil, why do you think Euphoria Rivers left town?"

"Don't know," Gil replied, scratching at the days-old stubble on his chin. Then a sheepish grin spread across his face. "Maybe it was the picture of her I left at the library." Gil thought his Black Beauty fly pattern looked stunning hooked through Euphoria's nose. Catch and release. That's the way to fish.

The Vengeance of Wiley Pescatoria

Robin Hillard

From the ferry dock, The Moonlight Bar cast an alluring light on the water of Quonsett Pond. Music drifted through the evening air, sprinkled with the laughter of holiday-makers enjoying the novelty of the pontoon restaurant.

Wiley Pescatoria ran a small charter boat, and found The Moonlight Bar a useful source of affluent vacationers. When four expensively casual, thirty-something males disembarked from the launch, he leaned on the bar and tapped his glass. "These ones look good," he said softly to Moonie, as the manager fixed his drink. "You've got your story straight?" Moonie nodded and went to greet the quartet.

"First time in Quonsettville?" he asked. Not idle conversation. Moonie needed to know the visitors were new in town, and their answer pleased him. He showed them to one of the popular window tables, where they could watch waves splashing against the edge of the pontoon. He personally delivered their drinks, asked about their vacation and found an opportunity to deliver his first line.

"That fellow could have a million bucks," he said pointing to Wiley, who did not look like a prospective millionaire. The strangers laughed their disbelief, and the manager left to talk to other customers. Later in the evening he came back, flourishing a laminated sheet with clippings dated ten years earlier.

"Robbery in Quonsett Cascade"
Thieves broke into the Nonesuch mansion on Bathilde Avenue. "They've taken my diamonds," a tearful Mignonette Nonesuch told our reporter, referring to the million-dollar Star necklace.

The second paragraph was dated the following day.

"The thieves responsible for last night's daring robbery were pulled out of Quonsett Pond. In the early hours of this morning two men were seen clinging to the hull of their overturned boat, which had drifted into a popular fishing spot. The diamonds are still at the bottom of the lake."

"We've all been searching for those stones," Moonie told them, "and that fellow could tell us where they are. He saw the boat turn over but he doesn't read the news, so he doesn't know about the diamonds. Last night he was boasting about his secret fishing spot. He won't say where it is because he thinks the other charter boats will take his customers. 'One skipper tried to edge me out,' he said, 'Ten years ago. I was doing some night fishing and saw a boat go belly up. Right on my spot.' He swears he would have rescued them, once the hull had drifted further out, but I'm not so sure. He's crazy about his secret fishing spot."

Moonie left the men to their drinks, but he knew they'd swallowed the bait.

The next morning Wiley was comfortably settled in front of his shack, reading the *Quonsettville Quacker,* when the party from The Moonlight Bar approached.

"Jeb, Louis, Thomas and McDuff," one said, pointing to his companions and, lastly, himself. "They say you know the best spot on the lake. And bring back the biggest fish. What do you charge for the day?"

Wiley named a price that would make most captains blush. "But I'm not going out today."

McDuff doubled the price, and before Wiley could answer his buddy tripled it. "It's our only time away from our wives," Jeb explained, "and we'd like to catch some really big fish."

Wiley reluctantly agreed to take them to "the best spot on the pond" and showed no interest when the fishermen, their fishing gear plastered with *Moonie's Bait and Tackle* stickers, wanted to "have a bit of fun" diving into the cold water. They spent most of their day on the bottom of the lake.

Wiley was delighted by the success of his scheme and imagined a season of lucrative charters. "With diamonds as bait we'll reel them in," he boasted to Moonie as he counted out the money between them. But that was their last big catch.

A few days later Moonie showed his laminated sheets to another group of visitors. They listened to his story, smiled in the right places and nodded at times, but made no effort to charter Wiley's boat. They knew something Wiley didn't.

Euphoria Rivers had spoiled the game. She'd finally completed her Quonsettville Historical Preservation League-sponsored book *The Story of Quonsettville*, and it included a description of the robbery, the plight of the thieves, and the success of the Vermont State Police SCUBA team, who'd recovered the Nonesuch necklace. Unfortunately for Wiley, Euphoria left copies of the book at every motel and camping ground.

So when the prospective victims read the tale, they knew the manager of The Moonlight Bar had set them up, and decided to have some fun at his expense.

The following night they returned to The Moonlight Bar, waving Euphoria's book and laughing at Moonie. "You local yokels must be pretty thick if you spent the last ten years diving for already found diamonds."

"Local yokel! Pretty thick!" Moonie seethed. Thanks to Wiley's ill-judged scheme, these sophisticated city folk made him the butt of their jokes. There was nothing he could say to the customers but next time he saw Wiley stepping onto the pontoon, he kicked Wiley out. "And don't come back!"

That was the end of Wiley's dream. The next morning, he sat on the deck of his unchartered boat, muttering into his beer and thinking of the money he had lost. Because of that book. Damn that Euphoria Rivers!

And there she was! Walking along the shore with her stupid dog. Wiley picked up one of the empty cans and hurled it at Clover. Fortunately for the dog, a morning of drinking had spoiled Wiley's aim.

Euphoria heard the dull thud of metal on the beach and turned to see Wiley swallow another beer. He crumpled the empty can and aimed at Clover again. And missed again.

"Trash!" she said loudly, pointing first at the can, then at the man on the boat. "Trash!"

Wiley raised his middle finger and swore in return, but Euphoria laughed at the insult, as if the boatman was beneath contempt. "Trash!"

That was no way to talk to Wiley Piscatoria! He'd make her sorry for insulting him and for spoiling his plans. He drank another beer and plotted revenge.

Every Sunday, Euphoria would park her Dodge Dart at the ferry dock and walk Clover along the lake to Gunnarson's Beach. She followed the path away from the lake as it wound through a screen of bushes to the off-leash area. There she would rest in the sun while Clover bounded through the undergrowth.

The following Sunday Wiley saw her old Dodge at the dock and guessed the direction of her walk.

Euphoria was surprised to see a familiar truck parked by the off-leash area. Wiley Pescatoria didn't have a dog, and if he had, he'd never make a special trip to give it exercise. He had not returned to his truck when she was ready to leave and whistled for Clover.

There was a scratching of the undergrowth, a startled yelp. The dog came running with her tail down and green splotches on her golden coat! The victim of a paintball gun! Euphoria stifled a gasp as she threw her arms around Clover, smearing her own dress with paint. She quickly hooked the leash onto Clover's collar and bustled away.

Wiley had made no effort to hide his truck, because he wanted Euphoria to know who'd marked her dog. When he drove back to the dock he waited, like an avenging god, to watch her bundle her miserable pet into her car. And to make sure she saw him. Let her rue the day she crossed Wiley Pescatoria.

Since Euphoria didn't know how her story affected Wiley's income, she saw his behavior as simply the nasty act of a nasty man. And nasties, like mosquitoes and sandflies, are part of nature.

What upset her most about that afternoon was her husband's reaction to Clover's ordeal. P.P. thought it was funny. "No harm done," he laughed, knowing it would be him who'd spend unpleasant hours scrubbing green splotches off the poor dog's coat.

"Beasts, the lot of them," Euphoria muttered, as she scribbled Wiley's name on the list that would later cause so much talk.

Another Job Well Done

Edward Andrew Parks

"Another fine day for plumbing," I exclaimed, stuck between pipes underneath a kitchen sink.

"Do you need something from the toolbox, Pa?" Freddie asked, a hint of worry in his voice.

"Nope, just trying to unscrew the pipe open so I can see what the problem is here."

"So, what *is* the problem exactly?" Mrs. Rivers asked, watching me with suspicion. Most likely she'd heard already I'm fresh out of prison.

Still, she needed a plumber on a Sunday, and I'm trying to build up Garfield's 7-Day Plumbing.

"Well, when I find out, you'll be the first person to know," I responded. "Just need to hurry this up so I can get Freddie back to my ex-wife on time. She gets a bit upset when I'm late."

She gets downright terrifying when I'm late, I thought to myself.

"Once you do find out, make sure you let me know," she said, as she sat down in her window seat, giving me a judgmental stare. She opened a book on her lap.

I struggled and wriggled out the screws from the pipe as best I could. After unscrewing two, a slight crack in the pipe opened up. A smell of sewage filled my nostrils.

"Ugh, that's a real bad stench in there all right," I exclaimed, covering my nose with my forearm.

"Can I smell too, Pa?" Freddie asked, as if I had taken a whiff of something appetizing.

"No, of course not!"

After slowly removing all the screws, I pried open the rusted pipe to find the culprit behind the clogging. A putrid odor blasted out, smothering my face.

"Oh Jesus Christ," I groaned with disgust, swallowing back the lunch I'd eaten two hours ago. I stopped breathing through my nose and let out a breath from my mouth.

I looked over at Mrs. Rivers, still sitting in the window seat, covering her nose with her book. "Oh!" she said, and standing up, headed for the back door. "I will be outside when you need me."

The door slammed behind her. I breathed out, then in again through my mouth.

Squinting, I peered into the pipe. I could barely make out what I was looking at. My eyes refocused, and I realized what I was peering at was a fatberg. A congealed mass of fat, oils, and grease, all hardened together to form a horrid abomination.

But now the real question was, how do I get rid of the damn thing? I know of fatbergs but I'd never actually encountered one, let alone had the pleasure of removing one. I slid myself out from under the kitchen sink, and stood up for what I hoped was a breath of fresh air, hoping an idea would pop up on how to remove this problem.

"What's under there, Pa?"

I put my arm around Freddie and brought him close to me.

"Something not of this world, Freddie," I said, still breathing through my mouth. "Something called a fatberg, a really nasty thing made from a combination of wastes that shouldn't have been flushed down the drain. And I don't know how long it's gonna take to get it out."

At that moment, a truly terrifying thought came to mind, the thought of what my ex-wife would do if Freddie got home late. "Oh shit!" I hissed, trying to hide the word from Freddie. This whole fatberg business would take too long to do right. And I feared the wrath of my ex-wife much more than the disdain of some old hag.

"Ok Freddie, so here's what we're gonna do!" I announced with enthusiasm. "You're going to go outside and tell Mrs. Rivers you want to play with her dog or something. And while you do that, I'll get rid of the fatberg. Got it?"

With a salute and smile, Freddie nodded his head and ran outside to Mrs. Rivers.

Time to get to work. I grabbed a kitchen towel hanging from a rail and tied it around my face, ready for round two. Positioned under the sink once more, I carefully went for a chunk of the heap of filth, grabbing into it with my bare hands. I realized my blunder in not using gloves as the revolting blob of sewage flopped into my hands. And there was a lot more of it still left in the pipe. It was as big as a rat, maybe two rats. Or an overgrown bog lemming.

Short on time, I scrambled up and with the kitchen towel still wrapped round my face, stood in the middle of the kitchen.

My ex-wife's threats to go to my probation officer if I'm late returning Freddie rang in my ears.

What do I do with the fatberg, I thought? And what do I do with the rest of the fatberg still stuck in the pipe? And what do I do when I have to get out of there in ten minutes to get Freddie home in time?

I scampered out of the kitchen, fatberg juice dripping from my hands. I ran around the house, searching for places to hide it, imagining my ex-wife calling my probation officer.

If this worked though, if I could find a good place to hide the fatberg, it was a win-win situation. I got Freddie home on time and the old hag got to smell shit for weeks.

As I bolted upstairs, I took a quick peak outside through the window on the landing. Freddie and Mrs. Rivers were still chatting outside. I ran up to the bedrooms with the fatberg wobbling in my hands. I quickly entered the main bedroom. I lay down, crawling underneath the queen-sized bed. I broke the fatberg into chunks, pressed it onto the wooden frame, hoping it would harden and stick.

Five, six, seven minutes passed, back and forth, removing more fatberg pieces from under the sink and sticking them under the bed. Just as I was about to step out of the kitchen, with the last fatberg piece in my hands, Mrs. Rivers entered from outside. With Freddie, who had a worried look on his face.

Time slowed as Mrs. Rivers and Freddie approached me. The last piece wobbled from side to side. I placed my hands behind my back and, looking around in a panic, I saw nowhere I could hide it without Mrs. Rivers noticing.

At least, not until a ray of hope appeared from the door behind them. Mrs. Rivers' golden retriever, Clover, ran into the house and bounding towards me, dashed around behind my back. The fatberg slipped from my hands. And Clover snatched it from the floor and raced off through the house with the last piece of fatberg between her teeth.

"What did you have in your hand, Mr. Garfield?" Mrs. Rivers asked.

"Oh, it's just a ... plumber's trick," I said. "Keep tasty treats in case you gotta deal with angry dogs."

I shrugged my shoulders and smiled. I looked over to my son. *It had to be done*, is what I tried to relay to him.

"Well, it's about time we got on our way," I told Mrs. Rivers. "You shouldn't have any more problems with your plumbing, maybe a slight lingering smell but nothing more."

"What was the problem exactly?" she asked.

"Oh, just a dead rat in the pipes. Or maybe a dead bog lemming, it was a bit hard to tell. Got rid of it already so don't bother checking for it." I gave a nervous chuckle.

I picked up my toolbox and, walking towards Freddie, placed my hand behind his back and pushed our way through to the door.

Outside, at a brisk pace, I helped Freddie onto the seat of the pick-up truck, stored the toolbox behind the cabin and looked back at Mrs. Rivers now standing on the front porch.

"It's been a real pleasure, Mrs. Rivers. I'll send you the bill in a day or two, bye now!"

I jumped into the pick-up and drove off into the sunset, another job well done.

I felt great. I got Freddie back home to his mother on time and she didn't call my probation officer on me. I was in the clear. I had succeeded in my mission. All was good.

At least until a few days later, when I received a very angry, and to be honest, surprisingly vulgar call from Mrs. Rivers, stating that she found the little 'surprises' I had left in her bedroom. Some of what she said to me sounded like something my ex-wife would say, and I didn't think she had it in her. Needless to say, I never received payment for that job and now, I've acquired the scorn of Mrs. Rivers.

Sunday Surprise

Tom Fegan

Pastor Michael Burton of Redeemer Bible Church: tall, slender and well-groomed, with coal black hair perfectly in place. Dark brown eyes accenting a smile filled with perfectly straight, pearly white teeth. Always friendly with a jovial humor about him; if only others could see him through my wife Euphoria's eyes. The truth might startle them.

"He's a charlatan, P.P.," she confided last Sunday afternoon. She'd been out walking Clover, our 18-month-old golden retriever. Pulling the rocker out so it blocked my view of a *Mannix* rerun, she dropped Clover's leash onto the floor and flopped into the rocker.

Euphoria is always right. When it comes to people, she has never made a wrong call.

"And what I saw today confirms it." Euphoria bent down and unhitched the leash from Clover's collar. Clover bounded up next to me and curled up on the couch. "While I was taking Clover for her walk along the pond, I witnessed it, with my very own eyes."

Quonsettville had grieved with Pastor Burton when his vibrant and stylish wife Jane had passed just a few months prior. The diagnosis: heart attack. She'd practiced yoga and was active in Euphoria's dance class at the community center – not 'Twinges in the Hinges', but her other dance class – so her sudden death was a shock to everyone in town.

Jane was a kind-hearted woman, and a beacon of our church. A picture of beauty, substance and class, she always wore her mid-brown hair piled on top of her head in what Euphoria always called "a slightly messy but still elegant if a little lopsided French twist."

This is a small community and we care for our own. And that includes blow-ins like a pastor and his wealthy-in-her-own-right wife.

"The Ladies League ladies all say Jane orders her clothes from a designer in Albany," Euphoria said one Saturday as we drove home after a wild-game church supper. "But that's unfair: when would Jane find the time to travel all the way to Albany?"

These are the facts of the case:

Jane was the only child of a wealthy Boston banking family. Or as she referred to it with a smile, "old money."

Her trust fund would revert back to her surviving relatives upon her death. And if she pre-deceased him, Pastor Burton would receive $250,000.

A pre-nuptial agreement was necessary for Pastor Burton to sign before the marriage was accepted by her parents.

And Jane Burton was so busy with her life as Pastor Burton's wife, she never had time to see her family.

Back in the rocker last Sunday, "Eyes are the passage to the soul," Euphoria chimed, like she frequently does, "and I can see beyond those eyes swimming in tears."

She rocked back and forth, once or twice.

"Pastor Burton is no more a pastor than I am a pasta *dish!*" she cried.

Much like our forty-nine-year marriage, Euphoria's position as Municipal Chief Librarian has established her as an institution in Quonsettville. She is a force to be reckoned with.

"Burton's eyes are cold and his smile is forced," she added. "He talks about Jane like she is an angel in Heaven but really, she is no more important to him than a game of pool at the Angry Squirrel Pool Room."

Quonsett Pond is murky and deception can run deep in a town of seven thousand people. Even more when there's not a lot to do in the tourist off-season.

It happened gradually, the presence of a woman dressed just like Jane, sitting in back at church.

"I am sure that's Valletta Vale," whispered Euphoria one Sunday morning, turning back to me as we sat in our usual pew: two from the front, alongside the center aisle. "She is a teacher of black arts and she has a class across the hall from me when I'm teaching 'Twinges in the Hinges'. But there she is dressed just like Jane, and she even has Jane's hairdo."

"A slightly messy but still elegant if a little lopsided French twist?" I asked.

"Now you are mocking me, P.P., and I won't have it," she whispered, tut-tutting me with her hand on my knee. "You know how perceptive I am about people. And Jane is my friend."

Valletta generally adorned herself in black, with her long black hair flowing down over her shoulders. She usually wore no makeup. I've seen her shopping for clothes in Diamante's Jeans Exchange.

But dressed like Pastor Burton's wife in church?

"Valletta's personal conferences with Pastor Burton in his office as well as the community center after classes have been noted by many of the Ladies League," Euphoria told me one night a few months back as we ate cider doughnuts while watching a rerun of *The Rockford Files*. "I saw Valletta after her class at the center tonight and confronted her."

I swallowed another cider doughnut whole.

"Naturally she denied everything," Euphoria continued. "*There is nothing to deny, Euphoria*, she said, like we were *colleagues*."

I licked my lips and said, "Things were so much better before Pastor Wells retired."

Euphoria nodded. She always enjoys my reminiscing about Pastor Wells.

"And when I called Jane on my cellphone, she dismissed it and claimed the meetings are an attempt to win Valletta over. Pastor Burton wants to neutralize what could be an explosive situation. You know, with her interest in black arts."

But back to Euphoria in the rocker. With me on the couch and Clover curled up beside me.

"Their faces were stuck together," Euphoria exclaimed, "on the edge of the pond during a time most people are busy and the pond vacant! They were still there when I drove by. I honked. They knew it was me!"

I nodded; her pink Dodge Dart is part of her identity. That's why it was easy convincing her to give her new electric Kia to our grandson Preston. She never *really* wanted a new car. Then she'd have to learn how to drive it, and she never has the time.

"Those green socks Pastor Burton wore to Jane's funeral and now seeing him with Valletta and her knowledge of black arts makes it conclusive that Jane was murdered!"

I was concerned about repercussions from Euphoria's drive-by action.

"What are *black arts* anyway?" I asked.

"Potions, spells, herbal medicines that those heretics do!" Euphoria exploded. "I do have access to such knowledge."

She glared at me.

I leaned over and ruffled Clover's fur.

"She can conjure up a poison, I am sure, enough to bring on a heart attack." Her face reddened as she sat back in the comfort chair. "$250,000 is a lot for someone not used to having money. That's for either of them as well as together!"

I peered around my wife at *Mannix* on the TV set.

"But no one in the Ladies League will believe me because they think Pastor Burton can do no wrong! And now *the pond* is ruined for me as well as *half the town*," she said. "I can't get that image of their locked lips out of my head!"

She dropped her face into her hands and shook her head from side to side.

"Poor Jane," she wailed. "Poor, *poor* Jane."

Yeah, I thought ... poor Jane.

originally published in

The Quonsettville Quacker, October 10th 2019

NEW CHIEF LIBRARIAN APPOINTED

by Local Political Reporter, Merriweather Rosenschultz

Following the sensationally abrupt departure of Mrs. Euphoria Rivers in June, and a subsequent exhaustive search to find a replacement, Town Clerk Daniel Dubonnet yesterday announced the appointment of a new Municipal Chief Librarian.

The new appointee is Mr. Theodore Waldmeister, of San Francisco.

"I have no previous connections to Quonsettville, nor to the entire state of Vermont," the new appointee said. "So I come to Quonsettville as fresh as a daisy."

Moving to Quonsettville will start a new chapter in Mr. Waldmeister's life. "I list my hobbies as leatherwork, needlepoint, and stimulating conversation," said Mr. Waldmeister. "And I am looking forward to extending my interests in all three."

Mr. Waldmeister leaves a responsible position as chief curator with the Castro Collection of Camp Curios. "But it's time to get back among the people," Mr. Waldmeister added.

Despite spending the last twenty-one years living in San Francisco, Mr. Waldmeister has not always lived a big city life.

"I was raised in New Hamburg county, Iowa, but I got out of nowheresville just as soon as I could," Mr. Waldmeister revealed. "But what it taught me is this: even cowtowns deserve some culture."

"Plus, I come from a family of ten, and we still all meet up at Thanksgiving and Christmas, so I have kept in touch with small communities that way."

What can Quonsettvillians expect with Mr. Waldmeister behind the library's front desk?

"Well, my college dissertation was on the role of the scream in silent horror movies, so I am hoping to start a golden years of cinema program."

And what of the touchy subject of extending library opening times to Sundays?

"My true intention is not just bringing people into the library, but bringing the library out to the people," Mr. Waldmeister said. "All options will be considered. After all, a community that reads together, stays together."

You can find Mr. Waldmeister behind the desk at the Quonsettville Municipal Library from Monday October 14th.

Also from Pure Slush Books

https://pureslush.com/store/

• Lust 7 Deadly Sins Vol. 1
ISBN: 978-1-925536-47-8 (paperback) / 978-1-925536-48-5 (eBook)
• Gluttony 7 Deadly Sins Vol. 2
ISBN: 978-1-925536-54-6 (paperback) / 978-1-925536-55-3 (eBook)
• Greed 7 Deadly Sins Vol. 3
ISBN: 978-1-925536-64-5 (paperback) / 978-1-925536-65-2 (eBook)
• Sloth 7 Deadly Sins Vol. 4
ISBN: 978-1-925536-66-9 (paperback) / 978-1-925536-67-6 (eBook)
• Wrath 7 Deadly Sins Vol. 5
ISBN: 978-1-925536-68-3 (paperback) / 978-1-925536-69-0 (eBook)
• Envy 7 Deadly Sins Vol. 6
ISBN: 978-1-925536-70-6 (paperback) / 978-1-925536-71-3 (eBook)

Also from Pure Slush Books

https://pureslush.com/store/

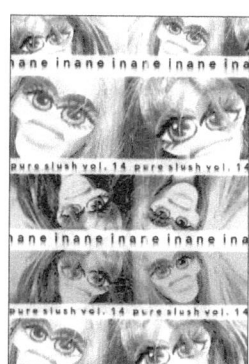

- Pride 7 Deadly Sins Vol. 7
ISBN: 978-1-925536-72-0 (paperback) / 978-1-925536-73-7 (eBook)
- Happy² Pure Slush Vol. 15
ISBN: 978-1-925536-39-3 (paperback) / 978-1-925536-40-9 (eBook)
- Inane Pure Slush Vol. 14
ISBN: 978-1-925536-17-1 (paperback) / 978-1-925536-18-8 (eBook)
- Freak Pure Slush Vol. 13
ISBN: 978-1-925536-16-4 (paperback) / 978-1-925536-15-7 (eBook)
- Summer Pure Slush Vol. 12
ISBN: 978-1-925536-13-3 (paperback) / 978-1-925536-14-0 (eBook)
- tall…ish Pure Slush Vol. 11
ISBN: 978-1-925101-80-5 (paperback) / 978-1-925101-98-0 (eBook)